The old man wanted to shriek and run. To fly. To roll and lope and tumble. Anything to escape. But the lunatic colors, the maddening vibrations, swirling and dancing, gathered around him like a wall. The tempo of the insane chorus rose like a high-pitched wail gradually climbing up the range of inaudibility: eddying, chattering, bellowing, until the old man threw his hands out in front of him and pitched forward into the roaring maelstrom!

THE
NEXT
ENCOUNTER

Donald Thompson

FAWCETT GOLD MEDAL • NEW YORK

THE NEXT ENCOUNTER

Published by Fawcett Gold Medal Books, CBS Educational and Professional Publishing, a division of CBS Inc.

ISBN: 0-449-14458-5

Printed in the United States of America

First Fawcett Gold Medal printing: March 1982

10 9 8 7 6 5 4 3 2 1

Dedicated to
Joan Comerford Thompson

THE
NEXT
ENCOUNTER

Prologue

The pine forest was dark and cool; it draped itself around the shore of the reservoir like a green lace collar. The trees were as evenly spaced as the columns of a cathedral. Up high, the top branches shouldered each other so tightly that they formed an umbrella through which the late morning July sun only pierced as single golden spears, casting hand prints on the ground; one here, another there.

An old man moved among the trees. He was tall, and as angular as a T-square. His face was leather. He had a full crop of white hair. He wore chocolate brown slacks, brown brogans, argyle socks, and an outrageously blazing Hawaiian sport shirt. Whenever he stepped into one of the shafts of sunlight his hair flashed silver. In his hand he carried a long stick which he used as a cane. He called it a tramping stick.

As he worked his way up the gradual incline away from the reservoir, sinking noiselessly into the soft carpet of pine needles underfoot, he wore a serene expression. The air was tingly against his face. His heart beat easily. His breathing was steady. He was in great shape for a man his age.

Near the crest of the incline he found a large, moss-covered log and sat down. He held the tramping stick across his knees. He savored the silence. He sat motionless, unblinking, as at home in the woods as a Mohawk Indian. Soon squirrels, at first alerted by his presence, began to galumph again. As did the chipmunks. Bird talk from the trees started again. The old man watched them with his peripheral vision; a tipped smile folded the corners of his mouth. When the creatures had grown sufficiently confident, he took some unshelled peanuts from his shirt pocket. He tossed them one by one.

"Here, ya little beggars, eat."

Up to this moment everything was what it had always been. The animals were eating. The filtered sunlight had its usual mystical cast. The stillness was broken only by the distant summer thunder of the big rigs out on Route 2.

Suddenly, there was an unfamiliar sound. Not a sound, really. It was the kind of deep earth rumble you feel in your belly rather than hear, like the explosion of an 81mm mortar shell with a delayed-action fuse. The chipmunks froze in the mouths of their burrows. The squirrels stopped, sat up, pointing their twiddling noses toward the sky.

The first change the old man noticed was in the air: it seemed to be subtly changing color. Its shadowed clarity was somehow misted over with a violet haze; dreamy, ancient, and alien. The old man seemed to feel the texture of the air on his arms like the sweep of an electric charge. His hands tightened on the stick. A squirrel across from him skittered up a tree.

The charged violet air washed over him. In the last

seconds before the feral fear blinded his brain, the old man thought he felt the violet air penetrate him.

His head was being squeezed. Sweet Jesus! What was happening to him? The shadows around him became malignant. The blots of sunlight became hideous cosmic pulsations. The summer breeze of a few moments ago cackled like witches' laughter through the trees. Every ganglion in his body became sensitized. For one awful moment he could sense the terror of the animals; he could hear the trees screaming!

And that color in the air. The soft violet it had been in the beginning had now blossomed into a swirling chromatic nightmare that leaped from tree to tree like St. Elmo's fire!

The old man wanted to shriek and run. To fly. To roll and lope and tumble. Anything to escape. But the lunatic colors, the maddening vibrations, swirling and dancing, gathered around him like a wall. The tempo of the insane chorus rose like a high-pitched wail, gradually climbing up to the range of inaudibility: eddying, chattering, bellowing, until the old man threw his hands out in front of him and pitched forward into the roaring maelstrom!

Chapter 1

*F*ran McCauley was home at last. For the first time since his plane had landed that morning, he was alone. Having showered for dinner, put on a fresh pair of slacks, a T-shirt, and a pair of desert boots, he sat quietly on the edge of the bed in his old room.

His sister, Palma, who was downstairs fussing over the cooking, had seen to it that nothing had been changed in the years that he had been away. His cherry wood desk stood expectantly in the light of its green-shaded lamp. Flanking the desk were his bookcases. On the left, the books that he had needed; texts, supplementary readings, his old copies of the Columbia Journalism Review: on the right side, the books he loved; Tolkien's *War Of The Rings*, Hemingway's *Torrents Of Spring*, Farrell, Fitzgerald, Robert Service, and Mark Twain.

Over the desk, in their eternal diving position, hung two model airplanes he had made in junior high: a

13

Spitfire and a Messerschmidt ME 109. The dope on their skins had long dried and cracked. Against the window an unpainted chest held all his old writing from high school and college. Some pieces had rejection slips stapled to them.

Fran was surprised at how small the room seemed. At one time it had been his whole world. He remembered being so small he had had to reach up to touch the light switch. He had imagined the room would be haunted by memories pressing to besiege him. Yet nothing happened. Perhaps later. Or perhaps he had just been gone too long.

He was only aware of today, as though his life had begun here in Watertown, Massachusetts this morning instead of thirty-one years ago. Palma had met him at the airport, gushing as usual. There had been the ride through Boston and Cambridge, then up Belmont Avenue. Even then there had been no flood of memories. Nothing had changed. Nothing does in New England. It almost seemed as if he had never left. The Handy Spa; the local bread, milk, and candy store, was still the same. The same teenage boys still hung out around the door: different kids, but still the same. The Marine Corps League Club, of which his grandfather was a member, was still there. Its windowless, low, stained wood structure still announcing that it was a *private* club.

A sudden, drumming knock battered the bedroom door.

"Hey, hey, in there! Are you decent?"

Palma came breezing into the room, her face shining with perspiration and happiness. She wore a flower print housedress covered by a full-sized apron.

"Boy, you're getting violent in your old age. First you try to strangle me at the airport with a hammerlock. Then you drag me all over town like the tail of a kite. Now you damn near knock down the door."

14

Palma giggled. "I'm just glad to see you, that's all. You'll just have to put up with me. After all, I haven't seen my baby brother in seven years. Are you ready for dinner? Oh, wait'll you see the roast. Five and a half pounds. I got Mr. Ronciewicz to give me the best one in the store. In ten minutes it'll be done to a turn."

Though brother and sister, Fran and Palma had little in common when it came to their appearance. He favored mother's people: medium height, dark curly hair and dark eyes. She favored the paternal side. Palma was tall and skinny. Her hair was red, her eyes blue, her face pale and angular. Dad used to say they were walking maps of the geography of Ireland. In the east, he would say, in Dublin and Wicklow counties, every second person looked like Palma. But in the west, thanks to the Spanish Armada's having washed up on the shore during the big storm, everybody looked like Fran.

"It's so good to have you back," Palma said, placing a hand on each of Fran's shoulders. Then she brightened again. "I'll bet it's all pretty dull for you, after the glamorous places you've been to. God! Rome. Bonn. Paris. London."

"Oh, sure. And don't forget those other glamorous places: Saigon, Cambodia, Indonesia, the Sinai Desert, and that gorgeous little radar station nine miles north of the air base in Keflavik, Iceland," he said.

"That doesn't matter. You've become a famous reporter, and that's what's important."

"A famous reporter?" he guffawed.

"Well? Gramps still carries around in his wallet the story that *Newsweek* magazine wrote about you."

"Oh, swell," Fran said. "Is that the one with the picture that shows me diving onto a helicopter on the roof of the embassy building in Saigon the day we pulled out? If I'm going to be famous, I'd like to be famous for something else besides that."

Like a mist, Palma's frivolity melted away. Again, she rested her hands on her brother's shoulder.

"Mom and Dad would be proud of you. Gramps and I are," she said. "You've made the whole thing worthwhile."

One of the old feelings stabbed Fran: guilt. *The whole thing* she had called it. What a masterpiece of euphemism. She was talking about *her* life.

Mom and Dad had moved into this house with Grampa when Fran and Palma were little kids, right after their grandmother's death. But when Palma was nineteen and Fran fourteen, Mom and Dad were killed in a car crash. Palma, whose sole ambition in life had been to marry and have a family, worked at a treadwater job then, while waiting for her white knight to come along. Their parents' death changed all that. Palma took on the responsibility of her brother; she found a job that would give her enough money to send her brother through school, and she put aside her own plans.

"I hope so," he said, squeezing his sister's hands.

"Oh, my God! The roast!"

Palma flashed out of the bedroom and clattered down the stairs. "Ten minutes!" she called behind her.

"Palmie, that was some dinner." Virgil McCauley looked at his grandson. "Makes you glad you come home. Am I right or wrong?"

"Don't ask me. You're the expert at paying compliments."

"I been eating her cooking longer than you have. Damn fool. Running all over the world when you could be home with a good cook like this."

"Look, Grampa. If I'd stayed home, I'd probably be married by now. And any girl I'd marry probably wouldn't be as good a cook as Palma."

"Hey, Little Brother, you're pretty good at the compliments, too. If you'll both just leave a generous tip

16

under the plates, the employees will appreciate it."
Palma folded her napkin in front of her and stood up.
"I'm going into the kitchen. Can I get anybody any-
thing? More coffee? Gramps, what about you? Franny?"

"Why don't you just sit down, for Christmas sake.
You're not exactly a waitress around here. Maybe we'd
like to talk to you."

"You can talk to me later. All I have to do is straighten
the kitchen a bit. It'll only take a minute. Besides,
after all that talking you did about how neat the
German women are, I don't want you thinking I'm a
slob. Sure I can't get anything?"

Both men indicated with pats to the appropriate
portions of their anatomies that they were stuffed to
the gunwales.

Fran and his grandfather rose heavily from their
chairs and lumbered into the living room as they heard
Palma begin her noisy puttering around the kitchen.
The summer air, as thick as the night, as warm as
gelatin, was redolent with the smell of cooked food.

"Funny how when you're hungry, ain't nothing smells
as good as cooking. But when you've eaten, the smell's
enough to turn your stomach," Virgil said.

Virgil dropped into his leatherette easy chair. Fran
sat on the sofa across the coffee table from him. The old
man offered his grandson a cigarette, then lighted it
for him.

"Ain't you afraid of smoking Camels? All the talk
about cancer and everything?" he said.

"I guess I am," said Fran, "but it's a matter of
priorities. With all the other things that are going on:
wars, revolutions, corruption, pollution, starvation, fam-
ine, and the possible threat of atomic incineration, it
seems to me that a guy who worries about cigarettes is
like a fellow making the Normandy landing who is
worried about catching athlete's foot in the water."

The old man laughed until he choked.

"Gotta watch that," he smiled after he had calmed. "I'm so damn full I'll be spilling over if I ain't careful."

He then reached over to the coffee table and picked up a carved wooden box. He opened it, and the plinky tune of *Lily Marlene* floated up.

"I thank you for the present. This is quite a curiosity."

"It's something to keep your marijuana in," Fran joked.

The old man did not respond. He continued as though his grandson hadn't spoken.

"Your father would have liked this. He kinda liked that song."

"I got it in Bonn. The Germans think it's the only German song an American would recognize."

Fran tried to imagine what the song meant to his father and to his grandfather. Even though he had traveled more than either of them, the song seemed to evoke images of distant places, of long-forgotten battles, of a part of history that he would never experience.

Both his father and grandfather had been Marines: Grampa had spent thirty years in, his Dad had helped take four Pacific islands during World War Two. Fran felt that Grampa had never forgiven him for taking a student deferment during the Vietnam War. Even though his first assignment had been a Marine fire base at Khe San, it didn't make any difference. By not wearing the uniform, he did not share a part of time with his forebears.

At the same time that these thoughts stirred from their cryonic vaults in his mind, Fran was observing his grandfather.

The old man sat forward in his chair, his elbows resting on his knees, like a fighter between rounds. The music box had fixed his attention. Fran noticed that a certain inexplicable change had impressed itself on him. His eyes still fixed, the old man's body became

18

tense. He tilted his head as though he were listening to a sound inaudible to anyone else, expectantly listening, a smear of dread shadowing the hollows of his eyes. Then, as if the sound he heard were the piping of some glen-haunted saraband, the old man's head began rhythmically rocking ever so slightly. For a full minute the young man was rapt by the vision.

"Grampa?"

"Yeah."

"You all right?"

"Why does everyone keep asking me if I'm all right?"

"No reason, Grampa. Just asking," said Fran.

The two men settled into a momentary silence. Grampa's face wore an expression of petulence common to the very young and the very old.

"Well," said the old man, breaking the silence, "how was things in Germany?"

"They were okay. The worst part of being a political correspondent is that no matter where you go, it's still the same place. The same plots. The same corruptions. The same big mouths. The thing I really noticed about Germany is that the people are almost pathologically clean. Their men's rooms in the public parks are cleaner than our hospitals. And they're so law abiding it's a fright to a good Boston boy."

Virgil laughed. His mood seemed to swing again.

"I guess they ain't changed, them Germans. Neat as a pin. Always was. I was in Germany after the First World's War. They was like that then."

"Since I've got you in the right time period, Grampa. I've been thinking I might do a think piece on the Prohibition Era. You're my great authority on such things. In those days, how seriously did people *really* take the Volstead Act, I mean with all the cops drinking in the speakeasies, and all?"

"Oh—about as serious as you fellows took your pot smoking in college. You pretty well knew you wasn't gonna get arrested 'less you did something to really rile the cops. Cops used it as an excuse to arrest you for something else. Cop wants to lock a man up, he'll always find a reason. 'Course, every once in a while there was a big raid that made all the newspapers. That was to please the pols. Just like you kids in the Sixties. I remember once . . ."

Virgil sat back, lit another Camel and began remembering. His stories had always been a high point in Fran's life. As far back as he could remember, Fran had been enthralled by the old man's adventures. Gramp's Prohibition-day tales were what had originally made Fran want to be a writer: he wanted to be able to put stories on paper with the charm Grampa had when he told them.

The old man had been a career Marine. Once the post-World War I German occupation was concluded, he was stationed at Boston Naval Hospital. Between his time spent there and two tours at the Boston Navy Yard, he had spent the better part of two decades in his own hometown. He had bought the Boston house, and had raised there his family, as though he were a civilian.

Gramps had known all the joints and speakeasies in Southie, Roxbury, and the South End, and, as far as Fran was concerned, the old man could outclass Damon Runyon for sheer whacky storytelling. He had drunk homemade booze called The White Death, or Grappa, or California Tornado. He had hung around with guys named Lop-Eared Harris, No-Balls Petrillo, Goose McGinty. God, what names!

If circumstances hadn't forced the issue, Fran might have left after high school, gone into the Marine Corps during Nam, then gone to New York to write novels and short stories. But Palma had worked so hard, sacrificed so much, that he felt duty bound to see to it that she hadn't done so for nothing. She had given up

20

her dreams of a home and children. He had given up his dreams of a cold water walk-up and a battered typewriter. He went into political journalism. Thanks to a boost from Darren Gilroy, he was hired by International News Bureau right after college.

But here he was at thirty-one, a recognized foreign correspondent, quoted by the local press, yet still wondering if he had done the right thing as he listened to his grandfather tell the old stories.

"All right, you two. Keep it clean. There's a lady present." Palma entered the room like a fresh breeze. She plopped down next to Fran, crossed her legs, and took a pack of Winstons from her apron pocket. "Now. What have I missed?"

"Not a goddam thing. Franny and me was just talking that old ragtime."

"Did you tell him about your accident?" she said.

"What accident?" Fran asked.

"The one he had two weeks ago."

"See that? Now you've got Franny all stirred up," Virgil said querulously.

"Maybe he ought to get stirred up. It's about time somebody talked some sense to you."

"I'm not stirred up, Grampa," Fran said. "I was just asking. What accident?"

"It wasn't no accident at all. That's your damned sister's idea, and she's as soft as a grape. I was just taking a walk in the old pine forest up by the reservoir. I got a little spell, that's all," Virgil said, making it sound offhand.

"A little spell! Listen to him. He *fainted*. He was unconscious for several minutes, at least. That's all," Palma said.

"I went to see that doctor of yours, didn't I? He said I was sound as a dollar, didn't he? Well, goddammit!"

"You shouldn't be hiking around in the pine forest anyway," Palma said, as though she were talking to a

21

small child. "A man your age. You'd think you'd have more sense. You're not twenty-one anymore."

The old man stood up angrily. "Well, you ain't either, for that matter. Ain't a goddam thing wrong with my age that people minding their own business wouldn't cure. It's a pity when everybody's concern for my health has got to ruin Franny's first night home. I'm going to bed. You two can discuss my health if you want. I'll see you in the morning!"

"But, Grampa. . . ." Fran began.

Fran's voice trailed off as the old man tromped off toward the stairway. He left only a bewildered silence behind him. Fran and Palma looked helplessly at each other.

"Now what the hell was all that about?" Fran asked, finally.

"Don't ask me," she answered. "He's been like that ever since that day he fainted in the woods. He's edgy. He gets upset over nothing. You saw it for yourself: all you have to do is ask him one question about his health and—bang—he goes right up the wall. Other times he gets depressed and he spends all day staring at the window. Sometimes he looks like he's listening for something. I don't know. It's beyond me."

"I know. I saw some of that 'listening' of his tonight. It's kind of scary. He almost looks like a different person. What's wrong with him? What did the doctor say?"

"The doctor said he was fine," Palma said.

"The doctor's crazy. There's something wrong with Grampa. How can he be fine when he seems almost to be undergoing some kind of personality change?"

"Don't ask me. The doctor says he's fine," said Palma, her voice confirming that the whole thing was beyond her.

"Could it be his age? I mean, could this be some form of senility?" said Fran.

22

"The doctor says no. He says he got the body and the mind of a man who's twenty-five years younger. Besides, you know the old Marine: the only way he'll die is to get run down by a truck."

Fran nodded in agreement, yet he couldn't shake the feeling of shadows being around his grandfather.

Chapter 2

The next afternoon the old man was having a beer in the basement bar of the Marine Corps League clubhouse. Franny had gone off to see some friends. The old man had just finished his third Budweiser when he noticed a certain *significance* to his head. He could think of no other way to describe the feeling. It felt as though a weighted band had constricted around his head at about the level of mid-forehead.

He looked deeply into the bar mirror facing him. But that was practically no help at all. Padney Flaherty had built shelves, three of them, right across the face of the mirror. "Why would you turkeys want to look at your pretty kissers?" he had said. Now three sentried rows of bottles separated the old man from the glass.

Still feeling the strange significance, he tilted his head, first one way, then the other, until he found a slot between a bottle of Canadian Club and a bottle of Old Fitzgerald. The fragmented face that looked back at him told him nothing. It was the same ol' Virgil McCauley, all right. Same old face: a mop of shocked white hair overlooking an unwrinkled but parchment-dry brow; cheeks that had lost their struggle with gravity, tight but not pinched, flesh a little empty looking, gathered into sagging dewlaps.

Second oldest member of the Detachment he was: eighty years old soon. Upstairs in the main meeting room there was a plaque honoring him.

McCAULEY, VIRGIL W. M/SGT. USMC RET.
1916—1946

NAVAL EXP. HAITI   1916
WORLD WAR I   1917—1918
  BELLEAU WOODS
  SOISSONS
  CHATEAU THIERRY
NAVAL EXP. HAITI   1920
US EXP. DOMINICAN REPUBLIC   1924
WORLD WAR II   1941—1945
  GAVUTU-TULAGI-GUADALCANAL
  GUAM
SILVER STAR, BRONZE STAR, PURPLE HEART.

No big deal, that plaque, Virgil thought. They give something like it to every guy who retires. Funny thing, though: a record like that makes you an old-timer. He had been a kid when he went into the Corps. He had run away from home at fifteen. Those days nobody cared too much about papers. You said you were eighteen, by God, you were eighteen. If you were big enough to walk, talk, crawl, and slap your ass with both hands, you could go. The old-timers to him then had been the guys from the Spanish-American War or the Boxer Rebellion. They were long gone now, all them guys. Yes, sir, old man time just walks along and don't give a big rat's ass for anybody. A familiar hollowness spread in his belly as he studied the sliver of glass.

Virgil had a little game he played by himself. He would stare intensely at his reflection then let his eyes go out of focus. Instead of sharply defined features he saw a rainbow blur. The beauty of the game was that you could superimpose on that blur any image you wanted. He noticed that his game-face appeared strangely mottled. A deep shadow cut across his eyes. He couldn't distinguish any object that would account for the weight he felt around his head, the thing that had started his musing. The sensation of weight, however, remained. That face. It was his, yet it was not. It was indefinably familiar—yet it was not. Goddam.

"Hey, Virg? You okay?"

Virgil snapped himself back into focus.

Joe Polito, the kid who had the bartending duty this week, asked from the far end of the bar where he was standing with Tracy, Kermit, and Foch. All good kids. Vietnam guys. Two bronze stars and four Purple Hearts among them.

"Fine and dandy," Virgil said. "Goddam. Everybody keeps asking me if I'm okay. My pants unzipped or something?"

"You're too quiet, that's all."

"Way to go, Virg. Keep this sonofabitch guessing," Tracy called.

"Tell him you're saving your strength for the disco tonight," said Foch.

"If you was any kind of bartender, Polito, you'd keep an eye on a man's drink and never mind how much he talks," Virgil bantered.

"There it is," said Polito. "No slack."

Polito slid another Budweiser down, skylarked a little more, then drifted back to his conversation with the others.

All regular lads, Virgil thought. And that was exactly what increased the hollow feeling inside him. Sure, they were good to him; sure, they respected him. They weren't peers, though. He had little in common with them, and having things in common was, for Christ's sake, what makes peers. There is among peers the ability to make a reference and have it immediately understood. One of these kids could say *Cam Ran Bay* or *Con Thien* and all the other kids would know what he was talking about. The older guys, the guys who had been in World War II, could say the *Slot* or *Shuri Castle*. But what about him? Oh, yeah, he had been in the Pacific, but he hadn't been in a line outfit, and he had just been treading water until the Marine Corps could get some younger guy to do his job. When he was on the Canal, he had been forty-one years old. After that he had been strictly administration.

He thought of his time as the First World War and a couple of campaigns during the 'twenties. Nobody was alive today in this outfit that remembered them days. There was poor old Jim Vanderveldt, and him on the way out, God have mercy on him. The burden of old age, Virgil thought, was the weight of the constantly explained references.

He whispered softly, *"Lucy de Bocage, Torcy, Chemin de Dame."* And smiled.

Another burden of old age, he thought, was that everybody thought you didn't have a brain in your head. He guessed they meant well, but what made them think you hadn't had a thought in forty years? Like his grandson, Franny, a big political reporter for one of them overseas wire services. Even Franny treated him like an old fart, like he couldn't carry on a decent conversation, so he got him talking that old Prohibition (Virgil pronounced it: Pro'bition) shit. Well, Virgil reckoned he could talk politics with the best of them.

He began to feel a tightness around his throat. He slid his fingers into the open collar of his shirt. Maybe he was getting too worked up with all this thinking. He swung around on the stool to face the television set in the back of the room, as if to break the mirror's spell. He was suddenly flushed with a new, inexplicable

27

sensation. For the veriest moment, the knotty pine wall seemed to be something else, some other fabric. What? Before he could be sure, the sensation passed. Had the walls really been the kind of splintery wood Virgil had imagined he had seen?

Tingles of fear climbed Virgil's spine. What the hell was happening to him? Was he having a heart attack? Was he getting senile? The grandkids were right, suspecting that he wasn't quite up to snuff. He had been acting goofy lately, and he knew it. He had been feeling goofy too. Goddammit. Maybe he was spending too much time living in the past.

What the hell else was there for him? He was an old man. He had been retired from the Corps for more years than most guys even put in. Nobody needed him anymore. His wife, Lord have mercy on her soul, was long dead. His only child was dead. His grandchildren were grown. One by one his friends had gone West. Who could blame him if he lived in the past? He was at an age where he could see things clearly.

Those years with his wife had been fine years, but there had been the responsibility and a lot of wrangling, the way married people wrangle. As he saw it now, the carefree years of his life, the happiest ones, had been the ones he had spent in the Corps as a kid. Not the fighting: the other things, the good friends, the drinking, the skylarking, the barbering. He had had more than friendship with these guys. Comradeship, by God! Maybe that was why he loved the Marine Corps League so much. All the voting members were former Marines. Maybe it gave him a sense of being back in the old days.

His ruminations were interrupted by a low rumble of thunder outside.

"I thought the weatherman said it was going to be clear today. Listen to that goddam thunder," he called to the other men at the bar.

The four looked questioningly at each other.

"What thunder?" Kermit asked.

"Oh, shit. You're so busy barbering you wouldn't hear thunder if it hit the building."

"Those weathermen are full of crap, anyhow," said Tracy.

Virgil gulped the last of his beer and slipped from the stool. As he walked to the door he felt a strange surge of youthful power in his legs.

"I gotta get on my way," he said.

"Going home?" Foch asked.

"Guess I better before it starts to rain."

"I hear Franny's coming home," said Polito.

"He's in already. Yesterday morning."

"Tell him to come on over. The first six beers are on me," said Polito.

"You know Franny?"

"For Christ's sake, Virg. Sure I do. You getting spacey? We went to St. Stephen's together. He was a senior when I was a sophomore. He used to drink here, didn't he? Wasn't he an associate member?"

Virgil smiled shyly. "I'll tell him," he said.

Tracy touched the old man on the shoulder. "Need a ride? I gotta get out of this rat's nest myself sooner or later. I can drop you off."

"Nah. Thanks. An old coot like me can use all the exercise he can get," Virgil said, shouldering the back door open, waving over his shoulder. The guys hooted warmly behind him.

Virgil stopped in the blindingly bright parking lot. The sky was cloudless, the sun murderously bright. Where the hell had all the thunder come from? As he walked, Virgil became aware that he had dropped into a slow, slogging gait, his shoulders hunched forward, his arms hanging and bent at the elbows. The surge of strength flowed through him again. What the hell's getting into me, he thought. His shadow reaching out in front of him seemed inscrutably changed. Yet it all looked familiar.

The feeling lasted until Virgil got to the park, and then as though the vigor of his youth had been transmuted to lead, the strange vitality drained out of him. He sat down on a bench under the full weight of his eighty years. He might have puzzled over the alternating changes within him, but his mind felt itself being shoved out of control. He clutched the edges of the bench with both hands as he felt himself slipping, slipping.

The universe was darkness, and without limit. No nearby object emanated an aura of biological presence. Out on its rim, no star rolled on in its own illuminated path. There was direction, a sense of movement, although there was no discernment of weight, no resistance, no point of reference. Time existed as insubstantially as the plane on which it functioned. At the final termination of eons, there was a line of cessation. There was solidity; distant, yes, but detectable. Then. Laughter.

The universe contracted itself into a single body of perception. The body rocked and shook.

"Virg! Hey, Virg! Wake up! Yo, Hurk! I found him. He's out here on the patio. Jesus Christ, look at him. He's pie-eyed. C'mere, will you? Give me a hand."

Virgil McCauley opened his eyes. The universe that a moment ago had been black, was now a scarlet haze. Two fuzzy outlines hovered above him.

"Well, well, what have we here?" said the outline called Hurk. "Sleeping Beauty awakens. A fucking prince must have kissed him."

As Virgil's vision came into focus, he felt a searing pain in his arm.

He groaned.

"Why should your arm hurt, stupid? Just because you get maggoty-assed and flop all over it?"

The figures became clear. Virgil looked from one to the other, puzzled.

30

"Verlager? Hurka?"

"Who the hell were you expecting, Isadora Duncan? C'mon, Dry-Balls, get up. You're too heavy to carry."

Virgil let himself be lifted by the two familiar young men and guided between them across the courtyard toward a noisy, musical, smoke-filled room. The two men were in their early twenties. Both were as tall as Virgil. One was lanky, the other was only this side of pudgy. They wore the shapeless forest green uniforms of World War I, with Marine Corps emblems in the high collars. Near the doorway, there was a mirror. Virgil jerked the little entourage to a halt. He stared into the glass with a sense of déjà vu. He, too, was tall and lanky, and *young*. His face was smooth and pale. He wore a uniform and his arm was bandaged.

"Let's get inside," said Verlager, "somebody's probably shagged our table as it is."

Inside was the crazy mash of an enlisted man's hangout, the Marines called them Slop-Chutes. The three gouged and elbowed their way through the mob of forest green, US Army OD; French blue, peasant blouses, and floor-length, rough-fibered skirts. The noise was deafening.

"Bet your sweet hind end the chickens are gone too," said Hurka.

Four French soldiers had taken over their table. The chickens were indeed gone. Under normal circumstances this invasion of their bailiwick would have led to a session of inordinate criticism. But, considering the three of them were on their first liberty from the hospital and were physically not quite up to snuff, it seemed the wiser course to share the table with the Frogs.

The waiter mauled his way over to them with a full tray. Verlager grabbed three glasses. One of the glasses he shoved over to Virgil.

"Cognac," he said. "Drink it. It's good for you. You

never could drink vin blanc," Verlager said, pronouncing it *vin blink* in the doughboy manner.

Virgil coughed and choked on the first gulp. The contents of his stomach churned, but stayed down.

"He's all right," said Hurka. "He's his same lovable self again."

"What did I do, pass out?"

"Pass out?" Verlager cackled. "You died."

"Boy, I must have. I had this crazy dream. I don't remember it, but it was so real. As real as hell."

"That's a bitch. That happens to me sometimes," said Hurka.

Verlager stood up.

"Now that things are normal again, I'm going to see if I can locate some chickens," he said.

"I'll keep laughing boy away from the vin blanc," said Hurka.

Chapter 3

*I*t was about ten that night when Virgil, loaded to the eyeballs, stumbled in the front door. Palma was waiting like an avenging angel. The old man had missed his dinner, he hadn't called, and she was worried to death. She raised holy hell. She had called the League Club, the Continental Bar, the police, the hospitals. Even the morgue. Where the hell had he been?

Virgil was impervious to his granddaughter's tirade. Fran sat on the sofa trying hard not to laugh.

"Look at you! You're drunk! I've never seen you so bad. It's about time you started acting your age. You have no consideration for anyone but yourself. Here's poor Franny waiting for you to come home. You haven't seen him in seven years, and while he sits here, you're out boozing!"

"Hey, Honey. . . ." Fran began, but Palma rolled on.

"Couldn't you at least have called? Oh, no. That's too much trouble. The streets are full of muggers and God knows what else, just looking for people like you. You could have been killed. You could have been hit by a car. I don't know what to do with you."

With that, Palma stalked off to the kitchen.

"If you want anything to eat, you can fix it yourself. Your dinner's in the fridge."

Virgil stood for a moment like a chastised boy. He looked helplessly at Fran, who was still suppressing his grins. Periodically, Palma poked her head from the kitchen to spear her grandfather with another imprecation.

Virgil stood weaving for another minute or so, then lurched toward the back of the house.

"Where you headed, Grampa?" Fran asked softly.

"Porch," the old man mumbled.

As the screen door slapped shut, Palma swept out of the kitchen.

"Where's the old fool going now?"

"To sit on the back porch for a while."

"He's incredible, just incredible," she said.

"Don't you think you may have come down a little too hard on him? Everybody gets stoned once in a while. Hell, he's old enough to drink if he wants to. Frankly, I think he's a trip."

Palma stared an icicle through her brother for a long moment. She lifted her eyes to heaven for guidance.

"Now listen to you! All set to defend the poor old man. What am I, the villain? You're as bad as he is. You're all nothing but little boys."

So saying, she stomped off again.

Fran was still grinning as he sat down next to his grandfather on the darkened porch. The air was sticky and warm.

"Looks like you really ripped it. Sorry you didn't invite me along."

Virgil let the words sink in deeply.

"Ah, Palmie's all right," he said thickly.

"Yeah she is. She was just worried, that's all."

34

The old man, his head fallen forward, was quiet for so long that Fran checked to see if he had fallen asleep. When he did look up his eyes were coals.

"Grampa, something's really eating at you and I think it's time you told me about it."

"Give me a cigarette," Virgil said.

As he lit it, soaking the tip, his body went through a series of shudders. When he spoke he did so with the exaggerated articulation of a drunk. He opened his mouth. His expression said he was about to take a step from which there would be no backtracking.

"I want to go to a psychiatrist," he said.

"What?"

"You and Palmie don't fool me. I know you're worried about me. I been acting kind of goofy. Am I right or wrong? I never thought too much about it. But Jesus Christ, something *is* wrong with me. I'm losing my mind. I want you to take me. Ain't got the guts to go alone. Besides, I don't want Palmie finding out. You know how she carries on."

Fran waited for the old man to continue.

"Know where I got drunk tonight?" Virgil asked.

"The club?"

The old man laughed a laugh that was only this side of hysteria.

"No. I got drunk at the *Pauve Manse*."

Virgil said it as though the name required no explanation.

"It's in Paris," he added.

"Paris, where?" said Fran.

"Jesus Christ! Can't you hear me? Paris. Paris. Paris, *France!*"

Fran's silence was expressive.

"As I stand before God. It's true. Don't you think I know what it sounds like? I swear it's true. I was sitting in the Marine League Club having a beer with a couple of the guys. I swear, I only had a couple of beers. I left about four-thirty. I wasn't drunk. I was feeling kind of funny, like that day in the woods, and I started to come home. I got to feeling tired, so I stopped in the park. Then, all of a sudden—bang!—I was there! In Paris. Really there. Only it wasn't today. It was sixty years ago!"

Virgil stopped. His voice had risen into a high register. He gripped himself for a moment, and went on in a voice that was almost a whisper.

He told Fran the story, from the time his friend had shaken him awake.

"Jesus Christ," Virgil sighed, "how could I have been there? How could Verlager have been there? He was killed by a one-pound shell three days before the war was over. Hurka died in 1955."

Another long pause.

Fran looked at his grandfather. Whatever the cause, the old man was in genuine distress. Fran picked his words carefully.

"Look, Grampa. You had some kind of an experience today, and you don't understand it. I can't say I understand it, either. But it doesn't mean you're psychotic. The human mind has a way of playing funny tricks. Sometimes it can make things appear to be something they're not. Your rational, conscious mind tells you that you couldn't possibly have been back in Paris on leave from the hospital after you'd been wounded. Yet something happened to make it seem as though it had happened.

"Who knows what the experience might have been, and who knows what might have caused it? I'll take you to a doctor if you really want to go. It might be a good idea. Not because you're psychotic—forget that— but to find out what kind of an emotional trauma you're going through. Once you know that, you're halfway to getting rid of it.

"You know, Grampa, you've had a couple of severe jolts recently, what with so many of your old friends dying. This might be some kind of subconscious response to their deaths. It doesn't mean you're losing your mind. You just might need a little help right now. Sooner or later, everybody does. We'll go off to the doctor tomorrow just to find out what's coming down. And there's no need to tell Palma about it."

Fran had been controlled and unemotional. To lighten the mood, he smiled. "Who knows? You might have fallen asleep on the park bench and dreamed the whole thing."

"Fell asleep, huh?" the old man sneered.

Slowly, with great deliberation, he unbuttoned his shirt cuff. He rolled the sleeve up to his bicep. He shoved his naked arm toward his grandson.

"Did I dream this, too?"

On the underside of Virgil's arm, even in the darkness, Fran could see a raggedly healing, angry, red gash that ran from mid-forearm to elbow.

Chapter 4

*T*he next day was Wednesday. It was a little after four o'clock in the afternoon as Fran and Virgil dropped at a table across from each other in the restaurant of the Statler Hilton, downstairs from the doctor's office. The hour hung heavily on their shoulders.

The waitress brought two coffees.

"You're looking tired, Boy," said Virgil. "This must be one hell of a vacation for you."

"I didn't sleep too well last night. Guess I'm not used to my old bed yet."

Fran was sure his grandfather understood the understatement. From the moment Virgil had lifted his sleeve, he had roamed the unlit living room. Sometimes he had thrown himself down on the sofa, but demon images racing around his head had always forced him up again. Sometimes he had sat on the sofa's edge, staring at the flowing designs on the old Persian rug. Periodically, he would go upstairs to check his sleeping grandfather, then return to the living room, stand before the picture window and study the emptiness of the street.

Now, he took a sip of coffee and reached for the sugar. Fran had been home a little more than forty-eight hours and things were certainly working out as he had planned.

"Well, there's no sense in beating around it. What did he say?" the old man asked.

"Who?"

"The doctor, who the hell are we talking about?"

"He says you're fine."

"C'mon. Cut the shit. I'm not a hysterical old biddy. We been all day in that shrink's office. He run more tests on me than I can count. Now tell me what's wrong with me."

"Nothing's wrong with you."

A flush of anger gathered under the old man's skin. Fran jumped in.

"Nothing, Grampa. And that's the truth. That's what he said. He says you're psychologically and emotionally well-pulled together. He said you have a firm grasp on reality."

"Then how. . . ?"

"He says," Fran continued, "your perception and control are superb. He said a lot of things, too, in psychiatric double talk, the bottom line of which is that you got a clean bill of health."

"Well, then. What about. . . ?"

"How the hell do I know, Grampa? I don't mean to be short with you. I guess I *am* tired. You asked me what he said, and I'm telling you. The whole business doesn't make any more sense to me than it does to you. I keep trying to talk to him about that scar of yours that's now an open wound. He mumbled some buzz words about psychosomatic disorders, and Christ knows what else. He looked at me as though I needed an examination."

"You telling me the truth, Franny?"

"You're so clean he didn't even recommend another visit."

There was no mistaking the relief on Virgil's face.

"What about the *Pauve Manse?* And Charlie Verlager, and Pete Hurka, and all them guys from the old outfit? What'd he say about that?" said Virgil.

"He says you probably fell asleep and dreamed it."

"Oh, bullshit!"

"You know, Grampa, you're absolutely right. I hope you don't mind my saying it because there's no point in worrying if we don't have anything to worry about, but goddammit, I agree with you. I haven't the faintest idea what happened to you in the park, but that scar is no dream. The incontrovertible fact is: a scar that has been healed for sixty years doesn't just suddenly revert to the original wound. He doesn't know, either, that's why all the double talk. I've been going nuts thinking about it, and I still can't get it to make sense."

"That psychiatrist sounds soft as a grape to me," Virgil said, as the waitress refilled their cups.

Fran sat back in the high-backed chair. He was smiling gently.

"I don't know if you have any idea how important that scar of yours is to me," he said. "I remember once when I was a kid—I couldn't have been more than six or seven—you took me down to the Public Garden to see the swan boats. We were over by the filtration pump where they have all those giant goldfish. I wanted to jump in the water and get one of them. You showed me your scar and said that's how you had gotten it: one of the goldfish had bitten you."

The two men laughed.

"No," said Virgil. "I don't remember that."

"I don't blame you. It wasn't exactly an earth-shaking incident."

Fran tried to imagine the day his grandfather had really gotten the wound, rushing a German machine gun nest near the railyards at Chateau Thierry. A

40

grenade splinter had sliced him as neatly as a surgical knife. The Silver Star had come later.

"Do you remember how I learned to use my little wooden ruler in the second grade by measuring that scar?"

Virgil nodded again, smiling.

Fran sipped. "Well, back to business," he said.

"Yeah, back to business," said the old man. "The doctor, what does he say we ought to do? I mean, do I have to take any pills or anything?"

"He says you could use a vacation. A complete change of scene."

"What the hell good would that do? If I got a problem because I'm getting old and I'm losing my friends, how the hell is going away going to change all that? You mean, if I go to Florida, say, I won't be eighty-years old anymore? Or Pete Karvanian won't be dead?"

"I wonder if it's really the worst idea in the world. How do you feel about it?"

"Taking a vacation?"

"Sure," Fran said. "Why not? It might not change things, but it could make you enjoy them more."

"Naw. It would be a waste of money."

"Look, Grampa, if that's a problem with you, don't worry about it. I've got a couple of bucks put away."

"Franny," Virgil said after a moment's thought, "it ain't that I don't appreciate what you're trying to do. I do. If I'm building up to some kind of problem—and I might be, no matter what that nutty doctor says—I'm better off right here on my own stomping grounds. Am I right or wrong? Your grandfather ain't a brave man but he's kind of stubborn. I been getting my teeth kicked in all my life because of it. I never run from nothing yet. I'm too old to start now. Does that make sense to you?"

Fran touched his grandfather's arm.

"Forget I mentioned it. Hey, it's about time we got home for dinner or Palma'll be climbing the wall again."

*   *   *

Dinner had been brighter than Palma had expected. Of course, the doctor's report was good news. Sitting on the side of her bed, the clock on the night table ticking with inordinate loudness, she thought of their laughter. Gramps and Franny had been flying, yet neither had had a drink downtown. The force of their joy had overpowered her fears. It was good to see them like that.

How different from when they had left the house this morning. Funny how going to the doctor had changed everything. Oh, they had made fun of the doctor at dinner. Gramps had called him a hot ticket. Yet the doctor's saying that nothing was wrong had somehow made it so. Like the priest in Confession, when he says, "Your sins are forgiven," and you feel all the guilt fall away.

She undressed and washed quickly, then threw on her pink cotton nightgown. She stretched out on top of the covers, which in this weather was only a sheet. She was tired. She thought of how busy she had been since Franny had come home; cleaning, cooking, and she thought how happy she was. Having her brother home had somehow pulled her life into shape. She had taken her two weeks vacation from her secretarial job, plus another two weeks without pay, and it seemed to her that all the work she was doing around the house *was* a real vacation.

She guessed that some women wanted careers, success, and recognition. That was all you read about in the magazines anymore. New life styles. Getting a bigger piece of the pie. She guessed it was all right for them. She was different and she wondered if it were a good thing. These other women who wanted so much seemed to get it. She wanted what was considered so little in life: a home, a family, a man, and she couldn't seem to get them. What was wrong?

42

Here she was now, thirty-six years old. There weren't any possibilities that she could see, and every day she got older, and just a little further away from the things she wanted.

Perhaps all the men had given up on her. There had been Claude Maxwell. He had wanted to marry her right out of high school. She had wanted to wait a few years. Then Mom and Dad's accident had happened.

A year or so later she had met Kenny Killian. He had been mad about her. She smiled to think of how he used to squirm when they were alone. She had had to turn him down because Franny had just entered college.

She checked an unbidden rise of bitterness. She loved her grandfather and her brother, God knows, but did something always have to come along to keep ruining her chances? Was she paying for some sin?

She smiled in the darkness to think of Richie Veneto. If ever there had been a sin, it had been Richie. Even thinking so didn't wipe away her smile. Franny and Gramps thought their little Palma was such a virgin. Wouldn't they be surprised? If that had been her sin, she would gladly have paid for it. There was no way she could convince herself that it had been. She had had a big fight with Father Quinlan over it in the Confessional. She would confess, she had said, but she could never honestly say she was sorry. At first he had tried to browbeat her. When that hadn't worked, the priest had bored her with a lecture on the differences between "actual" sorrow and "intellectual" sorrow. She never did feel sorry.

That, too, had fallen apart. Richie had gotten tired of waiting, like all the rest. She had read about his wedding in the *Globe* a year or so later.

Palma didn't want to go on thinking of the men who had stopped calling. She guessed there were enough women to give them what they wanted. A fist gripping her stomach forced her to admit that now she was the one tired of waiting. Thirty-six wasn't that old, but evidently her reputation as a stone wall had made the rounds.

She swore to herself by the power of the Sacred Heart, if she ever got another chance. . . .

Palma turned over in bed, crushing the pillow against her face. The house was quiet. Gramps was in bed. Franny had gone out for a while in her car. A few minutes ago she had been happy, now the old regrets were gnawing at her again. Funny how even a little happiness always smashed up on the rocks of her reality.

Fran pulled the car into the unlighted church parking lot. When he killed the lights and the motor, silent heaviness enclosed him. He lit a cigarette, wondering if Fr. Labordette would think he was crazy dropping around at this hour, asking the questions he was going to ask.

Crazy or not, Fran was too much of a reporter to let things rest where they were. He wouldn't do it if it were a story. Okay, the doctor had said Grampa was fine, but that still did not explain how the scar on Grampa's arm had suddenly reverted to the original wound. It also did not explain how a man with a rock-hard grasp on reality could believe with all his faculties that he had spent six hours in another time and place. Nor did it explain Fran's gut feeling that he was being drawn further and further down a dark hallway.

An aged, apple-faced caretaker wearing a dress left over from the McKinley era, led him to a quiet rectory waiting room. A modern crucifix hung on the left side of the door. The only other furnishings were three leatherette lounging chairs, a cheap desk with drawers only on one side of the knee space, and an ancient portrait of the *Last Supper* in a heavy wooden frame.

"For heaven's sake! Do I remember a Francis McCauley! What a question!"

Fr. William Labordette swished into the room, stirring a cool breeze with his Franciscan robe.

"One of the best editors we had at St. Stephen's. How could I forget? Francis, it's a joy to see you. Sit down. Can I get you a Coke?"

The priest was somewhere between fifty-five and sixty, and half-a-head taller than Fran, built like a polar bear. His hair had receded to an area around his upper ears, where it tufted out like bleached cotton.

There was much reminiscing about the old days at St. Stephen's High School, and the literary magazine that Fran had edited. They relaxed across the desk from each other as Fran brought him up to date.

"So you've finally decided to come visit your old ethics teacher," Labordette said, tactfully leading Fran to the purpose of the visit.

"Well, to tell you the truth, it's more than a social call."

"It usually is. As they say, it comes with the job. Nobody comes to see a priest unless he has a reason. One even doubts one's parents after a while."

"There's something you can help me with."

"Nothing serious? You haven't decided to become a Moonie at this late date?" The priest smiled.

"No, nothing like that. In fact, I didn't come to see you in your capacity as priest. I need some information and you happen to be something of an authority on parapsychology. If all that expensive education of mine taught me nothing else, it taught me where to go when I need help."

"You can try me," Labordette said, pleased with the recognition, pleased not to have to deal with a personal problem. "I have generally discovered that an 'authority' is a perfectly ordinary creature who is more than fifty miles from home. As you see, I live here."

Fran told the priest the details of his grandfather's illness, right up to tonight's dinner.

"You did the right thing taking him to a psychiatrist. Too many Catholics have the idea that a priest and a Confessional are some kind of homespun substitute. A priest's job is helping God save souls, not psychotherapy," Labordette said. "I don't see how I can help you."

"There is the matter of the scar."

"Yes. There is."

"I told you how well I know that scar. I'm not buying the doctor's story of psychosomatic disease or psychogenesis or psycho-anything-else. That scar is now a fresh wound. I'm damned well going to find out how it happened."

The priest sat back. He seemed to be pulling his thoughts together.

"I'm still not sure I can help you, Francis, but let me ask you if you've ever heard of Charles Fort."

"I know the name. He's a writer?"

"A writer, yes. A writer with rather a strange specialty. He started out as a newspaper man, maybe that's why you know the name. He made his reputation, however, with a series of books dealing with bizarre, factual incidents. He lived in the Bronx. He died, oh, somewhere in the middle 'thirties. I can't remember all his books—I believe he wrote four—his most important ones were *The Book Of The Damned* and *Wild Talents*.

"You see, he was born in the late nineteenth century and was raised during a time when science was spelled with a capital 'S.' Science had become so bloated with a sense of its own importance that it looked there for a while as though the lab might replace the church as the place where people came to worship. Fort wasn't so impressed. He observed that from time to time certain incidents occurred that science was at a loss to explain, and tended to sweep the matter under the rug.

"The significance of the title of his first work, *The Book Of The Damned*, was not as dramatic as it sounds.

46

He was referring to 'facts' which science damned to a world of silence."

"What sort of 'incidents' did he write about, Father?"

"Let's see. Frogs that rained down during a storm, for example. Or the Englishman who couldn't be hanged because a perfectly good gallows trapdoor wouldn't spring everytime he stepped on it. And—things like what happened to your grandfather."

"The scar, you mean? I don't understand."

"Not so much the scar, as the wound. According to Fort, things like it have happened. There's the story of the three Englishmen who each came into Charing Cross Hospital at different times during the day and night. Each had a slash wound on his neck. Each said he saw no assailant. And each claimed to have gotten it passing the same street corner. He has documented evidence that the same sort of thing happened in Bridgeport and New York City."

"You mean all these people just got slashed out of a clear blue sky? No assailant? No nothing?" Fran said.

"That's right. Oh, he has a litany of examples. I don't have the dates at my fingertips, but there were five or six stabbings in broad daylight in a Viennese restaurant. Somewhere around the turn of the century there was a rash of 'phantom' stabbings in Tokyo so widespread people thought they were being attacked by an invisible man or an invisible force."

Fran sat back. A smile tickled the corners of his mouth.

" 'Invisible man,' 'Phantom stabbings,' 'knife wounds' that just appear. Tell me straight, Father, what do you think of all this?"

"Understand, Francis, Charles Fort was a newspaper man. He had the same respect for *facts* that any newspaper man would. Yourself, for example. Every one of these incidents was taken from affidavits submitted by responsible people. Stories were run in responsible newspapers. I assure you, you have written stories with less confirmation than these. What do I personally think? I believe them."

Labordette was smiling, but firm.

"Okay, you believe in them. Let's say for a minute that I do, too. What does it mean? What kind of conclusions am I supposed to draw from all this?"

"Fort's point was that all sorts of things happen for which there are no scientific, rational answers."

"But, Father, that's crazy. Grampa is sitting in the park one day, minding his own business and suddenly a slash appears on his arm and you say nothing caused it!"

"Wait a minute," the priest said, "neither Charles Fort nor I said *nothing* caused it. Something we cannot explain with the current limitations of our scientific knowledge caused it."

Fran's doubts hung around him like clouds.

The priest continued. "Don't you see? There is a certain body of evidence that compels us to give at least a hearing to these incidents: affidavits by victims, affidavits by physicians, affidavits by eyewitnessess. The sort of 'proof' that would be acceptable in any American court.

"Even in our faith, Francis. What actual 'proof' do we have that a person such as Our Lord ever existed? What proof do we have that he made the lame walk, or the blind see? Or that he himself ever rose from the dead? Nothing but the accounts of people who claim to have seen it with their own eyes.

"Francis, unless we are prepared to say that *all* men are pathological liars, we have to give a certain credence to them."

Fran took the long way home. He drove through darkened Lexington, then around the reservoir.

If he had been confused before his visit to Fr. Labordette, he was boggled now. He had to admit the priest had a point: you have to believe people whose

48

judgment you trust. He, Labordette, was no fool. He had been a canon lawyer for years. He had written four well-respected, scientific books on parapsychology. You simply didn't dismiss his opinions.

Okay. So things happen we can't explain. Where did that leave Fran? Suppose he accepted the idea that there were weird, eerie, mysterious forces in the air that tear people up. Then what? The young man shook his head. No. He was just too pragmatic. Or else he was too close to the situation. All he knew was that something was happening to his grandfather and there had to be a better explanation than "forces in the air."

Chapter 5

*I*t was about midnight when Fran got home. A single lamp burned in the living room, otherwise the house was dark. A window air conditioner hummed tiredly. He went to the kitchen, ate a piece of cold chicken, drank a glass of milk. He smoked a leisurely cigarette in the living room without turning the lights up. His head was still heavy from his talk with Fr. Labordette. He felt himself in deep water, wrestling with his problem of reality. For all of it, though, he was not depressed. The doctor's positive diagnosis had had a more soothing effect than even he would admit. The house seemed a friendly place, the night relaxing. Even the problem itself seemed more academic than it might have.

He yawned. Roughing his hair with his fingertips, he headed for his bedroom. His tread was silent on the upstairs hall carpet as he passed his sister's closed door. He flicked on his light and closed the door behind him.

Virgil wakened slowly, like a bubble rising in a tar pool. He heard Fran's door close. He was conscious of a wink of illumination that peeped under his own door. Yet he wasn't sure it was this that had roused him. It was something more subtle. The old man wrapped his blanket around his shoulder, turned slowly toward the window. The same waking prod continued to jab at him. Slowly—very slowly—he opened his eyes.

And froze!

Two men were standing next to his bed. He blinked several times to assure himself that he *was* awake. A paralyzing fear kept him motionless. Virgil's skin turned to ice. His throat squeezed shut.

Before he could muster any response from himself, one of the men standing next to him spoke. The men were barely visible, both were dressed totally in black outfits that seemed to consist of slacks, a turtleneck, and ski masks. If their appearance was enough to freeze the old man, the voice was enough to make him shudder. It was raspy, almost a buzz. It seemed to articulate its words in a manner impossible for the human mechanism. It seemed not to come from a single source, but rather to fill the room simultaneously. It had no identifiable accent. It was, however, so heavy with scrupulous precision that it was obvious the language was not natural. There was an alien chill to it, almost more than Virgil could bear.

"Please do not be alarmed. You must get dressed and accompany us," the stranger said.

The second figure moved toward the foot of the bed with an oddly disjointed motion.

"Who. . . ?" Virgil whispered.

"You must not be afraid. We have not come to harm you. It would not be possible for us to explain ourselves to you in any manner that would be comprehensible. Let it simply be said that we are emissaries on an important mission. It is essential that our mission remain completely secret. That is why we have come to visit you like this. You must rise and accompany us. You will be gone only a few hours. You will be returned unharmed before your family awakens."

The gentle words were strange. As he spoke them, the stranger, and his companion, emanated a malignant menace as thickly as a murky tarn emanates miasma. Virgil could feel, not see, a pair of fiery eyes piercing the darkness.

"I ain't going nowheres. Why should I go with you?"

The speaker remained silent for a long while.

"I repeat: it would be impossible for us to explain ourselves in any way that you would accept. Since you require an explanation in exchange for your co-operation, let it simply be said that within your sphere quadrant it would be said that we are crew members of what would be called an Unidentified Flying Object."

He didn't speak again for a moment, to give Virgil a chance to absorb what had already been said. Then he continued.

"There is a program of progressive advancement among a number of planetary units of which your race is, at the moment, unaware. It may not at the moment be explained to you. However, there has been an unforeseen malfunction which we have been dispatched to adjust. You are inadvertantly involved. You cannot sense it yet, but you are in danger. You must come with us—for treatment."

The intruder seemed to be selecting his words carefully. Virgil's ears relayed the message to his brain, where it was summarily rejected. Crew member? UFOs? Since he had opened his eyes, Virgil had felt no sense of reality about his midnight visitors, as though his world of sleep had somehow extended itself beyond his eyes. Another incident in the dizzy phantasmagoria that had been swirling about him lately.

He waited in silence for, perhaps, a laugh, some

indication that these two birds were hoods, and that they were ribbing him.

Again the intruder picked his words.

"You have been exposed to certain radiations. They have caused the inexplicable phenomena you have noticed about yourself lately. What we propose is a simple process. It will be painless. You will be returned to your home immediately."

The frozen tundra within the old man suddenly turned to lava.

"I think you guys are nuts! What the hell are you bullshitting me for? You want to rob the house, well, goddammit, rob the house. I ain't young enough to stop you anymore. But just because I'm old, don't think I'm nuts, or that you're going to pull my leg. Whatever you're going to do, you'd better do it in a hurry, 'cause in about ten seconds I'm going to start raising hell. I'll have every cop in the world all over you!"

"Mr. McCauley, please. You must keep calm."

Again the reasonable words were accompanied by scarlet hatred.

"We understand that the very fact of our presence is difficult for you to comprehend. In a similar position, given your background, I would feel the same way. Mr. McCauley, there are certain things you must accept because we tell you. For example, the malfunction of which we spoke is much more serious than you can grasp. It would be comparable, within your frame of reference, to your having contracted a virulent and extremely communicable disease. Not the same, not truly comparable, but correct in a broad sense.

"Not only is this 'disease' a threat to you personally. Unless it is corrected immediately, it will become a menace to your entire race. It is easily 'curable' at this moment. It must not, however, be allowed to continue for another hour. You could not even begin to grasp the consequences."

Virgil found himself wavering. What kind of a nut

53

was this guy? What a crazy story. Yet he was so sincere, Virgil might have gone along for the gag except for one thing that wasn't a gag: the sheer alienness of the man, a coldness of *unlife*, a thing chilling beyond mere physical death.

As his eyes became more used to wakefulness, Virgil could discern beneath the deep shadows that covered his face, the man's porcine features, or at least the outline of them. That emanation of hatred washed over the old man again and galvanized him.

"I ain't going nowhere with nobody. Now get the hell out of here and do it quick!"

The figure at the foot of the bed spoke for the first time.

"You must. There is no choice. You can not be permitted to transmit your infection."

The figure at his side produced a hand-held device the likes of which Virgil had never seen before, and gestured with it.

"Please, Mr. McCauley, come."

The old man snaked out a hand toward the lamp on the night table.

Glass shattered. Virgil bellowed. Feet scuffled. Grunts and howls, muffled by the closed bedroom door, thumped out into the hallway. A chair was flung. Bodies thudded against walls.

"Oh, God! What's happening!" Palma shrieked as she flew out of her room.

She was summarily pushed out of the way by Fran, hurtling himself toward his grandfather's door. He tore it open. Silhouetted against the window, he saw three dark, grappling figures, one of which was his grandfather! The old man's breath wheezed like a bellows as he flailed against the other two. From behind Fran, Palma screamed loudly and continuously.

Fran waded in. He jerked one of the black figures loose and let him have both fists. His victim, caught off-guard, reeled. Fran attacked and pounded him to

54

the wall. A stunning electric shock from behind slammed Fran to the floor. The second figure shoved Virgil to the bed. To his companion he shouted something in a foreign language that Fran heard only vaguely. Another whack stunned Fran to a moment's unconsciousness. But that was all it took.

Palma gathered herself enough to switch on the overhead lights. The sudden burst of illumination showed the final instant of the intruders' departure out the window. Fran could not pursue them. He had only recovered himself enough to lift himself to his hands and knees.

"Gramps! Oh, Gramps!" Palma screamed, rushing toward her grandfather's prostrate body.

Fran rose, and he too stumbled toward the bed. He rested a hand on Palma's shoulder. "Palma," Fran gasped, "call the cops. Grampa? Are you all right?"

"Yeah. Yeah," came the stetoric reply.

Virgil lifted his head. His eyes were fiery pinpoints: eyes that had looked on Gehenna. His skin was pale and damp. When he spoke, his voice was a ghastly rale from deep inside. He speared Fran with his stare. His lips moved, but at first they uttered no sound.

Later, reedy words would allow themselves to be formed.

Chapter 6

*T*he police left at dawn. Fran walked with the two officers out to their car, while the embryo sun tinted the first outlines of trees and roof tops.

"If you remember anything else about what they looked like, it'd help. 'Two White-Male-Adults' ain't much to go on, but we'll do what we can," the older of the two cops said.

"I'll try," Fran said. "But as I told you before, things got moving around pretty fast and I didn't get much of a chance to look at them."

"Paramedic says that's a funny wound you've got on your head. He's never seen nothing like it," the older cop said.

"Feels funny, too," Fran said, touching the small bandage and grinning sourly.

"That grandfather of yours must be made out of iron," the younger cop said. "The paramedic told us he was in great shape, except for being shaken up a bit."

"He's a tough old turkey," Fran said.

Palma stood in the doorway clutching her robe to her breast. She had said goodbye to the last of the neighbors who had come over to see what the rumpus was all about. Looking at Virgil collapsed in his easy chair, she sighed. Then, as though she had just remembered something, she scooted into the kitchen to pour from the new pot of coffee she had made. By the time she returned, carrying three mugs on a wooden cutting board that she used as a tray, Fran had come in and had closed the door behind him. All the strangers had left the McCauleys' private world.

Poor Franny, she thought. He looks exhausted. Some vacation for him. He would have been better off staying in Germany.

"Here," she said, serving the coffee. "It's fresh. I can't believe it. It's just incredible. We could have been killed in our beds. Those people are animals. What did they expect to steal from *this* house?"

Fran studied his grandfather's expression. It had changed only in degree from upstairs. His lips were held tightly together. His eyes dull. He had grunted short answers to the policemen's questions, and it was obvious he intended to tell Fran and Palma little more.

Fran gave his sister a significant nod.

"Well," she said, having gotten the message. "You two can thrash this out. I've had more than enough. I'm going upstairs. Maybe I can get a little rest."

A silence settled between the men after she had left. Once or twice Virgil looked as though he might speak, then changed his mind, lowering his chin.

"Look, Grampa, we're not going to get anywhere until you start talking to me."

"What am I supposed to talk about?"

"There's more to this than there seems to be, isn't there?"

The old man didn't answer.

"I know you, Grampa. I know when you're getting cagey."

The old man shot him a hostile look, but remained silent.

Fran continued. "I've covered enough stories to be able to develop a smell. I know when a guy is trying to keep his secrets. Something happened in that bedroom before I got there, didn't it? And you don't want to tell me about it. You trusted me about that thing in the park and I didn't let you down. How come you don't trust me now?"

There was anguish in Virgil's face. Fran had never seen the old chestnut so close to cracking.

"Those guys didn't break into the house to rip it off, did they?" the young reporter persisted.

Silence.

"Rip-off artists, at least those in their right minds, don't break into a house when they know people are home. Do they, Grampa?"

No answer.

"They wait until the house is empty," Fran said, pointedly.

"Franny. . . ."

"Who were those guys, Grampa?"

Virgil shook his head.

"Whoever they were, they were after you, weren't they?"

His grandfather lowered his head, nodded yes.

"Jesus Christ, Grampa? What did they want from you? What're you keeping it such a big secret for? I think you *do* know them. They didn't just drop in from a clear, blue sky."

Virgil laughed bitterly at these words.

"Come on, Grampa. Goddammit. Tell me."

"Franny, let me ask you something. Could you lend me some of that money you said you had put away?"

"Sure. But what's that got to do with what we're talking about?"

"I was thinking I'd like to go on that vacation."

There was an edge in Virgil's voice that Fran couldn't identify.

"Why the sudden change of heart about vacations?"

"I'd just like to go, that's all," Virgil said, querulously.

"Where do you want to go?"

"Anywhere. Just away."

Fran leaned over in the elbows-on-knees position he had learned from his grandfather and sipped his coffee. He reached a tough decision.

"Okay. You've had your fun, Grampa. You're either going to tell me what went on in the bedroom before I got there, or I'm going to beat it out of you with a wet noodle. You're running from somebody. You won't tell me who they are or what they want. Come on, Grampa. We're both too old to be jiving each other like this. I'm as hardnosed as you are. I've had a lot of practice these last couple of months. I am going to find out, Grampa, and you might as well understand that. Now who were these guys and what did they want?"

Virgil spread his hands in a gesture of surrender.

"Okay," he said, "you want to know, I'll tell you."

"A flying saucer? Oh, Dear God," Palma said, her face more resigned than shocked, Fran thought. Her hands remained still, one on top of the other on the kitchen table.

"It's been coming. I could see it coming. Poor Gramps," she said.

Palma had just returned from an afternoon of grocery shopping. Since the incident during the night, she felt that she had lost her grip on the one thing that had held her life together: her grandfather. Whether good or bad, it had been her life, now it seemed to be slipping away.

She had bought party food for tonight's dinner, a grim attempt to ignore reality. Coming in, she had noticed her brother sitting alone in the breakfast nook, smoking and nursing a cup of Maxim.

"Not out gadding about?" she had asked.

The ashtray in front of Fran was glutted with dead, bug-like cigarette butts. They had made more inconsequential talk as though a certain space had to be filled before they could say the words that had to be said.

Then Fran told her what Virgil had said.

"So the doctor was wrong. It looked as though things might work out, but deep inside, I had a feeling," Palma said.

"They don't look good now," her brother agreed.

"What does it mean?" she asked.

"I haven't the faintest idea. I've been sitting here for quite a while and all my mind does is go around in circles. Grampa's gone down to the League Club. I'm supposed to pick him up later. I don't know what that flying saucer business means but I do know you and I have to make some serious decisions."

"How much did Gramps tell you?"

"Just about what I told you."

"Is he telling the truth?" she asked.

"He's not lying, if that's what you mean."

Palma played with her fingers as though she expected to get some answer from them.

"Dear God," she said. "I wonder what's wrong."

"There are a couple of ways of looking at it. What do you know about paranoid schizophrenia?"

"That's like a split personality, isn't it?" she said.

"Yeah. But that's an oversimplification. I did a piece on it once. It's a hell of a disease. Even the doctors aren't sure whether it's psychological, emotional, or chemical. I got a pretty good rundown on it.

"There are different kinds of schizophrenia. There's one type called catatonic that turns you into a silent, staring vegetable. There's another type that turns you into a giggler. The one we're concerned with is paranoid.

"The doctors say this is the problem that develops

when the problems in your life become too much to bear. Your mind becomes active, and creates other problems to distract you, or to give you a message, anything to relieve the pressure. Paranoid schizophrenics are the ones who 'hear the voices,' and see the 'men from Mars.' They find people in the next room who are trying to wipe out the world with a death ray."

"And you think Gramps. . . ?"

"I told you I don't know what to think. I'm just trying to make sense out of a problem. I may be off my rocker. I mean, the psychiatrist downtown didn't see any paranoid schizophrenia.

"Anyhow, the doctors I talked to when I was doing the article claim that paranoid schizophrenics begin seeing things and hearing voices, and no matter how outrageous these visions might be to the individual, they all have three things in common. First of all, the vision or the voice is always something or somebody that the patient *could* believe in. A science fiction fan, for example, might see a nine-eyed Man From Mars. A deeply religious person might see Jesus. You see?

"Secondly, these hallucinations are always authority figures, someone of great power, somebody you wouldn't argue with.

"Third, they, the authority figures, are always involved in some kind of plot or experiment with the victim."

"And you're saying. . . ."

"Palma, for God's sake, don't make it any tougher for me than it is. It *does* sound familiar, doesn't it? First he tells us these burglars are from a flying saucer. He says they weren't trying to steal anything. They wanted him to go to their 'ship' with them. See the plot? They say there was an 'accident' and now Grampa has to be 'deprogramed' or he's going to be a menace to the whole human race. He talks about their having an 'atmosphere' of hatred. Admit it, Palma, these are classic symptoms."

61

"Those men in his room were real enough. You got hit by one of them," she said.

"Aw, come on, Palma. Are you being purposely dense? I didn't say the *men* weren't real. What they weren't is men from a flying saucer. That's the whole point. I'm sorry I jumped at you like that. You're as confused as I am. Consider this. Something has been working on Grampa for a couple of weeks now. Right? Something has been bothering him pretty badly. Maybe all it took was these two guys breaking into his room to push him over the edge.

"Think about it. Where would he get the idea of an 'accident?' Isn't that what you've been needling him about ever since he had that attack in the woods? You and I keep calling it an 'accident.' Maybe we planted it in his subconscious. Maybe the idea got worming around inside his head and one day came out as something else. Symbolism. That's classical paranoid schizophrenia, too."

"What about the scar on his arm you keep talking about?" Palma said.

Fran slid out of the nook and began pacing the kitchen. The scar. Grampa's trip in time. Fr. Labordette's Fortean explanation. Another link in a chain of things that just can't happen, but do.

"Jesus Christ, Palma! I don't know. Every time I try to string some facts together so that they make sense, they fall apart somewhere along the line. But it's got to make sense.

"Look. You don't really believe Grampa was back in France, do you? Do you believe in time travel? Do you believe those guys who broke into his room were spacemen? There has to be a way to explain this. There has to be a way to help Grampa. Frankly, the only thing that comes near to it is the paranoid schizophrenia theory."

"The psychiatrist said he was okay," Palma said, evenly.

62

"I know. What the hell am I, some kind of villain around here?"

"What do you think we ought to do?" she asked.

"What do *I* think? When did I start making decisions around here? You're the big sister."

"And you're the man in the family now. Whether you like it or not. I'll go along with anything you say," Palma said.

"What the hell kind of a cop-out is that? You've been making all the decisions for the last fifteen years. Why do I suddenly jump in now?"

Palma's voice was steady and cold.

"Maybe that's the problem. Maybe I've been making the decisions for too long now. I'm tired of making decisions. You do it. It's only fair. It's your turn. I'll decide what to have for dinner. I'll figure the family budget. *You* can decide the big things for a change."

Fran stared at his sister for a long moment. For the first time he saw clearly the tired thirty-six-year-old woman in front of him. He walked over to her and kissed her on top of the head. Then he dropped back into his seat at the nook.

"Sorry. I guess it *is* my turn. I haven't been thinking." He lit another in his chain of cigarettes.

"All right," he continued, "for what it's worth I think Grampa needs professional help. I think paranoid schizophrenia is a real possibility here."

"Do you think we should commit him?"

"Jesus, don't say it like that. You sound like a prosecuting attorney. Maybe we can get him into some kind of private hospital."

He thought her eyes were flaying him.

"I mean," he said, "it's something we have to do. It's for his own good. The way he's going, he's going to kill himself. Don't you agree?"

Palma only nodded her head, but when she did, the expression he had originally taken for serenity chilled him.

"Give me the keys to the car, will you?" he said, rising. "I'm going down to the club to pick him up."

Fran eased over into the right lane of Belmont Street, his right turn signal clicking like a metronome.

Most of the traffic, shiny and hot in the glare of the late afternoon summer sun, was moving in the opposite direction: from Boston toward the suburbs. It was just as well for Fran. Only a fraction of his mind was on his driving.

He saw his grandfather's face reflected in the objects around him, and the more he saw it, the more his determination wavered. Here he was on the way to confront the old man, to tell him that he was incompetent, and belonged in a private hospital. Fran could see clearly that old face wrench with the shock of betrayal. Here was the man who had raised Fran since his parents' death, now having his right of choice taken away from him as though he were a child.

And how could Fran be so sure? The old man seemed to have all the symptoms of paranoid schizophrenia, yet a doctor had not seen it, as long ago as the last couple of days. Then there was Fr. Labordette who had assured him that there were things in this world that had no logical, scientific explanations.

He approached the clubhouse, tapped the brake, and swung slowly into the driveway leading to the rear parking lot. The buildings crowded him.

So intent was Fran on navigating the alley, so deep into his personal travail, that he barely looked above the hood. At the end of the alley, the engine suddenly died. *Then* he looked up. And froze.

Standing motionless at the end of the buildings, one on each side of him, were the two men who had broken into Grampa's room last night! Something more than the black clothing they wore, which even in daylight seemed to be shrouded in an uncanny mist, made Fran certain they were the same men. He felt, again, the red

64

bolt of hatred he had felt the night of the struggle. It seemed to emanate from the figure on the left as he pointed a hand-held, box-like device directly at the engine. Had Fran not gripped himself, he felt he would have been swept away by the hate.

An instant later, the encounter broke off. The engine jumped back to life. The two men had disappeared as though they had never existed.

Inside the club, Fran moved through the social room. Distractedly he answered greetings, returned hand shakes, and backslaps. He found his grandfather sitting in his usual seat, talking to John Gavigan. Virgil looked intently into Fran's face and seemed to see something. He sat back expectantly. It took the young man a few minutes to work Virgil loose, away from conversation.

Fran softly whispered into his grandfather's ear, "Let's go home and pack, Grampa. We're going on that vacation."

Chapter 7

*T*hey fled from Watertown at midnight. Virgil, Fran, and Palma were piled into the car and shot along the Masspike, on their way to New York. Fear was a hound behind them. The night outside, redolent with humid summer heat, was hostile, and strangely chilled. It pushed against the windows. It hissed with serpentine menace around the hood ornament, up from the grill, along the air scoops. The lights along the highway were graveyard sentries, posted in pools of iridescent mist. Inside the car, the humans drew primal comfort from each other's company.

Palma drove. Her brother sat in the passenger seat next to her. Her grandfather was in back with the luggage.

"I can't believe it," she said, breaking the silence. "I mean, London, Paris, Dublin. It's incredible. It's like a dream. I know it's old hat to you guys. All the traveling around you do. But I never thought it would happen to me: that I'd be going to faraway places."

The men did not respond.

In the rush of packing, after they had come back from the Marine Corps League clubhouse, they had not explained much to her. What, in fact, *could* they have explained? A flush of danger that Fran had detected from two total strangers? A fear in its rawest form, so strong that he dragged his family away into a self-imposed exile? Even now, as they ran, Fran was still not sure what he was running from.

Palma already knew her grandfather was troubled, and had seen the men who had broken into the house. Men—or whatever they were. Fran thought it best to let her just extrapolate from there. A few *facts*, tightly held, could be a comfort.

At one point, he had taken her aside and had told her that he had decided on a vacation as sort of a last chance before sending Grampa to a psychiatric nursing home. To see if he improved any. Evidently, it was enough to square the earlier conversation she had had with her brother.

Fran looked across at his sister. The paleness of her face in the reflected light of the headlight beams, seemed to symbolize the swamp of terror he felt them in at the moment. He envied her innocence.

"I like it even better that we're leaving from New York. It would be fun to leave from Boston, but New York seems more appropriate, you know? Like the vacation has already started before we take off."

"That's not why we're going to New York," said Virgil, dully, his voice hollow from the cave of the back seat.

"Oh, I know. Franny explained it to me. It's because of the passports. We can get them quicker in New York, right?" she said to Fran.

"That's right. All we have to do is buy the tickets. Then show up at Immigration."

"You know me," Palma smiled. "I'm like a little kid. I love to talk about it. Packing was such a mess, I hope

67

we have all the papers. What are we going to do about Gramps's birth certificate? He doesn't have one, you know. They didn't give birth certificates when he was born. Not in Woburn, anyhow. They got him listed on the census for 1900. You think that'll be enough?"

"If it isn't, we'll write up a couple of affidavits. Besides, we've got his retirement certificate from the Marine Corps. That ought to do it," Fran said.

"You guys sure do change your minds in a hurry. One minute we're not going anywhere, then the next minute you've got me packing bags."

Palma chuckled to herself, then lapsed into silence. From the expression in her eyes, she was living her fantasies out in front of the car, the headlights playing on them like spotlights.

Fran's thoughts, meanwhile, poked around the events of the last couple of days, like a hound sniffling for an opening in a fence. He resented Palma's expecting some cogent response from him while his brain wanted only to wallow in the despair of the flight from Watertown.

As he looked at Palma it reminded him of how much things had changed since his plane had let down in Boston less than a hundred hours ago. And it seemed more pronounced since her hair was tied back the same way it had been. She was wearing the same kind of pink, cotton, sleeveless dress she had worn at the airport to meet him.

"All this talk about New York," Virgil said. "What I want to know is what we're going to do when we get there."

Fran was surprised. The old man hadn't spoken three sentences since they had left Massachusetts.

"So, you're awake," he said.

"I'm awake all right. I been doing a lot of thinking back here," Virgil said.

"If you've got anything good going on in your head," Fran said, "let me in on it."

"I ain't got a clue. But I'm just wondering if all this running is going to do any good. You can't run forever. You gotta stop sometime and make a fight of it."

Fran looked at his sister. He wondered what the old man had on his mind. Whether it would upset what little equilibrium Palma was adding to the family by letting her know the true nature of their "vacation."

"Okay, Grampa. I agree with you I'd like a couple of answers to a couple of basic ques .ons before I start swinging. Like: 'Do you have the slightest idea who or what we're fighting?,' or 'What are we supposed to fight *with*?' "

Fran was annoyed at the sharpness in his own voice.

"I ain't got a goddam clue, if you want to know the truth."

Fran softened his tone. "I don't think we have to run forever. I think what we need is a breather. We have to get away so we can get a little time to think. To learn something. Then we can get this business straightened out."

"Like how?" Virgil said.

"We could start by talking. I know some people in New York who should be kind of knowledgeable on the subject. Maybe we can read some things. I don't know. We'll just play it by ear."

Virgil paus d for a long while.

"Franny," he said, "you really believe them fellows was off a flying saucer?"

"Shit, I don't know. Do you?"

Virgil laughed. "See," he said, "they got us believing, almost. That's quite a curiosity."

In New York, during the false dawn, they found rooms in the Cabana Hotel, over on the west side. No easy project in New York during the summer if you don't have reservations. Virgil and Fran shared a double. Palma had a room to herself.

It was now five o'clock. Virgil was asleep. Fran stood

alone in front of the window, looking over Eleventh Avenue toward the Hudson River and New Jersey. Even from the tenth floor, he could hear the grinding of the garbage collection trucks below. The first automobile lights crept out on the roads across the river. The air conditioner hummed in the room. The window stood between Fran and the onset of the kind of summer day New Yorkers call a *scorcher*.

At first, he looked at the city lovingly: the thousand buildings, the streets and alleys. A human-made forest. A thousand, thousand places to hide. He felt a great familiarity with the city. After all, this city, and many like it, were his natural habitat. After the last seven years where would he be more at home than in a strange room in a strange building? Didn't he belong with the transient smells? The disinfectants from the bathroom, the laundry smell of the bedding? What else had he known since he had left home?

With the familiarity came relaxation. The danger dampened down. His brain seemed to creak loose from the numbing fear that had locked it.

He looked at his grandfather. The old guy was zonked. His features were serene. His breathing even. Virgil seemed to know with his body that they had passed through the danger zone. The tiredness that was upon him was the healthy, youthful kind.

Or was it? For an instant Fran wondered if his grandfather might not be in another of his trances. A flash of cold passed through the young man. No. He looked again. Grampa was sleeping.

Fran turned back to the city. Tomorrow, something would begin. What? he wondered. It might turn out to be a bizarre hunt in which the hunted hunted for a defense to fight back against the hunters. Fran suddenly realized what an ugly, primitive word *hunt* was.

His mind and body both were becoming too relaxed to confront the problem of where he would start. He could only ride with the emotion of knowing that his grandfather was a walking alien bomb, set to detonate at some unknown moment. When would he drop into another trance? Would it be like the last one? Would it be worse? Or different? What would be the result of the next one? Death, perhaps. The aliens had said Virgil's "disease" was fatal. Perhaps insanity.

The distant sky over Fran's shoulder was smudged with gray as he turned to his bed. He didn't know how yet, but he'd think of something—tomorrow.

Chapter 8

*T*en-thirty the next morning, Fran and Palma and Virgil split up on the Fifth Avenue side of Rockefeller Center. Fran went south; Palma and Virgil went north. The sun was already attacking with all four paws. A few minutes later, Fran shoved his way through the glass doors of the International News Bureau on the eleventh floor of the Schuyler Building. He dropped his employee ID card on the desk of a young receptionist, whose blouse wasn't quite unbuttoned down to her belt.

She pushed a button and spoke a few words into an intercom. A young man, slightly older than Fran, sailed out of one of the offices flanking the foyer, his face split by a grin, his hand extended. He was mustached. He wore a pink shirt and a red tie beneath a flapping, opened vest.

"Well, all right!" he boomed, pumping Fran's hand.

"Francis McCauley: The Voice of Bonn! What the hell are you doing here?"

"Vacation. Or at least that's what it started out to be. I'm squiring my sister and my grandfather around town. Last time I saw this office was the day I was hired. So I thought, since I'm in the neighborhood—*wuhyee not?* And, who knows, you guys may be able to help me with a project."

The receptionist, who had gotten no hint of Fran's status from his ID card, looked up curiously.

"Mara, this is Fran McCauley. It's his stuff you unwrap from Bonn, Germany, sometimes. He's a hellova guy. We did some time in Nam together before I got respectable. He's single, too."

"Ah, come on," the young woman said, shaking hands.

"Be careful of him. He's the serious type. He's going to be our own personal Ernest Hemingway someday."

The young man guided Fran into his office.

"You should have told us you were coming. We'd have had a big bash. This way you'll just have to settle for lunch at *Michael's*."

His name was John Lynker. He was a former field reporter who'd shown some talent for administration and had been tapped for the front office two years ago. Eight years in Southeast Asia and a demanding new wife had convinced him to take the job.

Lynker punched his intercom. "Mara, anybody calls for me, I'm out until I tell you otherwise. Okay?" To Fran he said, "You'll never believe who's here." He hit another button. "Duck into my office for minute, will you? I've got a surprise."

Fran shot out of his chair when a woman, about twenty-five, stepped through the inner door. She wore a white cotton blouse, gathered at the neck and a severely cut ecru skirt.

"Balls of Christ!" she said, throwing her arms around Fran. "Not you, too?"

"Eloise Courtney!"

"Fan-tastic!" she said.

"You know, if I had thought all day I couldn't have thought of a righter person to show up than you," Fran said.

"I'm flattered. Lynk, are you going to serve some of that bilious coffee or are we going to die of thirst?" she said.

The bantering was over in a few minutes. The catching-up took a little longer. By eleven-thirty they were on their second cup of coffee. Fran was amazed at how much Eloise had changed. She had been a green kid out of college when he had broken her in three years ago in Bonn. She had become self-assured since then, and had acquired that witty cynicism that seemed to be the characteristic of all print newspeople.

These were friends. Even so, Fran very delicately got around to his point.

"I think it's a hell of an idea:" Eloise said. "Doing a really definitive book on UFOs. I think we need one. Thanks for thinking I'm an expert, but you're going to have to dig a lot deeper than what I know."

"You did a piece on Saucers last year, didn't you?" Lynker said.

"Yeah," Eloise answered, "but it was mostly a political angle. This outfit in Arizona, called itself *Ground Saucer Watch*, brought suit against the CIA and the FBI under the Freedom of Information Act, and found out that a lot of information had been withheld. It was just another hit on the CIA and the FBI for all their secrecy over the last fifteen or twenty years." To Fran she said, "This is what's going to make your book a major project, if you intend to do it right. You've got so many different angles to approach it."

"Like what?" Fran said.

"Oh, like politics to start out with. Sure, people have

74

been reporting sightings for centuries, but remember the real plethora came during and right after World War Two. That was cold war time. The government got involved in it almost immediately. Washington spent a lot of effort trying to convince the American people that it was nothing more than a kind of mass hysteria. But actually, they were kind of worried that it was some kind of German or Russian secret weapon. I can give you what notes I have. You can dig from there."

Fran had his notebook flattened out on the corner of Lynk's desk. When she paused, he looked up. "Okay, what else?"

"Then, I guess, you've got to do some heavy historical research. These things have been being spotted for years. Nobody until our time called them UFOs, but you'll find all sorts of references to 'fiery chariots in the sky,' and what not. You'll find them in the damndest places, too. In the Bible, for example. Check the Book of Ezekiel. You'll find all sorts of references in the Hindu scriptures. *And,* you might remember, they've been sighted in every country on earth. So you're going to have to check a lot of international records. My piece wasn't so extensive, it was only a magazine article, so I didn't bother."

Fran continued scribbling.

"Then, I think, you're going to have to consider the good Mr. von Daniken."

"I know the name," Fran said, "but I can't place it."

"He's a writer. He did a thing called *Chariots Of The Gods?*. It turned out to be a best seller. It made him as rich as German chocolate cake."

"Not that nut! He's as crazy as a bedbug. A couple of interviewers have torn him to shreds. What a phony. You don't believe anything he says, do you? He did it for money," Lynk sneered.

Fran looked at Eloise to see how she would answer.

"Now, hold it. Just a damned minute," she said. "I concede there is some serious doubt about the guy's sincerity today. I concede, too, that his last couple of books are as full of holes as a politician's speeches. Think about this, though. When he wrote *Chariots* he was a poor slob working in a hotel in Switzerland. He did all the research out of his own pocket. Who the hell knew this kind of book was going to become a best seller?

"If you recall, his author's introduction was a masterpiece of scientific objectivity. He said something to the effect that he wasn't trying to shove anything down anyone's throat. That he had come up with this theory and he wanted people just to think about it. That's all: think about it. He said, I think correctly, that you never make any scientific advancement if you don't have a theory as a starting point. Okay. So his theory was pretty far out. As far as I'm concerned, it makes as much sense as anyone else's—on a subject about which nobody really *knows* anything.

"When the book became a best seller, this poor, poverty-ridden dude suddenly finds himself with money in every pocket. Then a big American TV network offers him a mil to come on camera and put on a show. So he does. Wouldn't you? If someone gave you a mil? I agree his later stuff was strictly for the bread. All that crap about caves full of gold."

Eloise slugged from her coffee cup as Lynk grinned in defeat.

"For a mil I guess I'd do a hell of a lot," he said.

Fran said, "You people are way ahead of me. What theory? To say the least, I've never been particularly interested in flying saucers."

"What theory?" Lynk mimicked. "Look at the man from Mars."

"Von Daniken said that a long time ago—a *long* time ago—back when people were cuddly little creatures living in the trees, or in the caves, or wherever, that a UFO, or UFOs, landed on earth. The primitive humans, being as primitive as they were, thought the spacemen were gods. Now the spacemen, not being gods: being about as fallible as creatures can be, and having been a long time out in the void, took some of the primitive females out into the bushes. And the results of these first gracious little sortees became the type of human beings that we are today. Half-animal and half-celestial.

"These spacemen were just decent enough that they kept checking back throughout the development of their children. In fact, they even helped with the development. Hence, all the references to them in our religious literature. Von Daniken says, whenever you read about angels, they're talking about spacemen. Interestingly enough, he points out that *angels,* as a concept, are common to every culture on earth."

"So are vampires," Lynk said.

"Don't be such a goddam cynic. I find it just as easy to believe in spacemen as I do in angels," she smiled.

"Another question." Fran wanted to walk delicately around this one. "Do you know any case of these UFO spacemen ever getting mixed up with people? I mean, verifiable people. Somebody I could talk to?"

"No. Absolutely not. There are all kinds of stories floating around in the tabloids. You know: *A Spaceman Kidnapped My Family.* And, *A Spaceman Is My Baby's Father.* That sort of crap. Just tabloid stuff. As far as genuine cases of contact between humans and UFOs are concerned, there's not a single example, with hard evidence, of any contact."

Lynk stood up from behind his desk.

"No more questions. It's time for lunch."

Eloise and Fran stood. Fran closed his notebook.

"You know what his problem is, don't you?" Eloise said to Fran. "He can't stand an intelligent conversation. He's just like the rest of these newsmen: all he wants to do is gossip."

"Come on. Let's go. We've got the rest of the afternoon for you two to have intelligent conversations. Me: I'm hungry."

Chapter 9

*L*unch at *Michael's* wrapped up about four o'clock. After long goodbyes, Eloise and Lynk returned to the office. Fran worked his way down Avenue Of The Americas to 42nd Street. There he turned left to the Main Public Library on the corner of Fifth Avenue. He felt completely mellowed out. Walking up the front steps to the main entrance, between the crouching marble lions, he felt almost foolish about his mission. His head was buzzing with all the UFO talk. His pockets were bulging with the bibliographical notes Eloise had given him.

At the banks of card catologues, he got the information on three of the books. He hoped these would tell him most of what he wanted to know. Time was short. They had to be on the plane tomorrow night. He carried the card information to the call window and waited for his number to come up.

In the cathedral-like reference reading room he sat

at one of the long tables and paged through the books. He was unable to concentrate. The words tumbled around in front of him.

The feeling of foolishness that he had experienced earlier now returned, even more forcefully. What in the name of God did he hope to get from the books? He remembered Eloise had said she had never heard of an example of a UFO having gotten mixed up in an individual's life. If she had never heard of it, it must never have been written. For all her modesty, her knowledge seemed encyclopedic.

That's why the two of them had been such a good team in Bonn a few years ago: she had been a dynamite researcher, with a memory like a tombstone; he had been the creative writer. He slowly closed the book in front of him. No. He guessed he didn't need anything he was likely to find in it. His problem was too personal. Even at that he wasn't sure just exactly what the dimensions of the problem were. All he really knew was that a couple of far-out guys who claimed to be from a UFO were trying to deprogram his grandfather from a "disease" they said he had. It seemed hopeless to learn anything from reading. He suspected he and his small family would have to deal with the aliens as the circumstances arose.

He thought more about Eloise. There had never been anything between them. As he thought about the good times they had had together, he let his eyes wander to the gargoyles on the balcony latticework high overhead, at the giant volumes, and found himself staring at a man sitting at the end of the table with his head propped in his hands. Why hadn't Fran trusted Eloise at lunch? He could have told her everything. Of course, Lynk had been there. He imagined what Lynk would have said!

Fran suddenly wanted to leave the library. He wanted to spend a night without worry. Without decisions to make. He stood up quickly. As he did, he noticed the

80

man at the end of the table was staring at him now. Embarrassed, Fran wondered if he had said anything aloud, which he sometimes did when he was in deep thought.

Out in the hallway, Fran found a bank of public telephones.

"Hi, Eloise. Yeah, it must be at least forty-five minutes since I've seen you. Right. Listen, if you're not busy with Robert Redford tonight, why don't you let me spoil you? Let's have some dinner. Any place you'd like. We're rich. Sure. Okay. I'll pick you up at the office. Be right there."

He hung up. Deposited another dime, and dialed again.

"Look," he said, "I want to leave a message for Mr. Virgil McCauley, Room 1021. This is his grandson. Tell him I'm having dinner with a friend of mine from the office. I don't know what time I'll be home. Got it?"

The clerk repeated the message.

"Okay. Thanks," Fran said.

Eloise insisted they go to her apartment before they went out to dinner. She hung his cord jacket in the closet. She sat him on the sofa, then presented him with a dish of iced raw carrot slices and a spritzer.

"I pick my friends that way," she said. "Anybody who eats the raw carrots is never invited back. The spritzer is so trendy I can't believe it. I guess there's no sense living in New York if you can't be trendy."

She disappeared into the bedroom. In a few minutes Fran heard a shower running.

Every square inch of Eloise's living room wall was covered with bookcases. Poking around, he realized how orderly she was, and how well-rounded. The books were grouped by subject: history here, public policy there, humor, novels and poetry. He was mildly disappointed to find she had no section on UFOs. In this instant of reacquainting himself with Eloise, he knew

81

he had to tell her. She had the kind of mind that could give him direction. She was as orderly about everything as she was about the filing of her books. He was exactly the opposite, and knew he needed the balance she offered.

When Eloise returned to the living room, her hair was still damp around the fringes. She wore a casual dress, flat shoes, and a single strand of pearls.

After dinner they hung over their brandy.

"Are you still up for spoiling me?" Eloise said.

"That's what we're here for."

"And we're still rich?"

"Sure."

"Good," she said. "How do you feel about going out and doing some dancing dancing?"

Fran smiled. "Dancing dancing?"

"Yeah. The stuff that's left over after all the disco dancing and boogie dancing, et al, is out of the way. You know, that old fashioned boy–girl stuff people used to do."

"Oh," he laughed, "dancing dancing. You know a good place?"

"I like Under The Clock at the Biltmore."

"That's good enough for me. Old-fashioned dancing dancing seems pretty appropriate after all the reminiscing we've been doing," Fran said.

"That's not exactly what I had in mind. I have to cheer you up."

"Why? Do I look as though I need it?"

"Need it?" she said. "You look like the guy who just found out his vacation relief man did a great job," she said. "You and I have known each other for quite a while now. I guess I know you well enough to know when something is bothering you."

"If I tell you, you may well think I'm off my rocker," he said. "It's quite a story."

"That's all right. I never thought you were all in one

piece upstairs, anyhow," Eloise said, signaling the waiter to bring another brandy.

"Why don't you light another one of those disgusting cigarettes that are ruining your health, and get started?" she said. "We can do our dancing dancing later. You don't have to get up in the morning. You're on vacation. And I'm so used to going into work wiped out, I'll never notice."

"For one thing," Fran began, "I'm not really doing a book on UFOs. I had other reasons for wanting information."

"That's no big surprise. I didn't think you were. You might write a book about Boston during the Prohibition years or about the loneliness of unfound love, but never about UFOs. It's not your schtick."

Through two cigarettes and most of the brandy, Fran told her. The experienced interviewer, Eloise listened. From time to time she jabbed with germaine questions.

"There it is. If you don't believe a word of it I wouldn't blame you. But you have to meet these guys. You have to be around them to feel the bad vibes. I'm open to any ideas you have."

"You really feel that there's more to this than the random incidents that Father Labordette was telling you about?"

"Well," he said, "there seems to be a pattern. Don't you think so?"

"There seems to be. What with your grandfather's experience; with the two guys breaking into your house; with their hanging around your grandfather's club. I can't figure what the pattern might be, unless, of course, they're telling you the truth about this 'plague.' It seems to me that nobody's giving enough thought to that. Suppose they are telling the truth, Franny? Wouldn't it be worth the taking an hour to have them do their 'deprograming' and getting the whole business out of the way?"

"I thought about that," Fran said. "But these aliens,

as I told you, are something else. They just exude hate. I just don't want to take a chance on what their idea of 'deprograming' might entail."

"I don't know. It was their motivation in the first place. What kind of preparations to guard your grandfather have you made in New York?"

Fran's face went blank.

"You're not doing anything," Eloise said.

"Why? How the hell are they going to find us in a city the size of New York? We could lose them in the crowds."

"Oh, you dimbulb. Think about it. If these people are really from a UFO, the last thing they need is some kind of public exposure. Yet they think your grandfather's 'plague' is so important, they're taking a chance on it. Do you think they're going to fold up their tents just because you ran away from Watertown? Forget it. In fact, if we can suspend our disbelief a little further, we can assume that they're going to be even more persistent. Don't think the crowds in New York are going to stop them, it's just going to make them more sneaky. If we can assume that they are aliens, who have the power to traverse the solar system, is it wrong to assume that they have other powers that we don't know anything about? As much as I love it, I can't imagine what you're doing here with me tonight."

Again Fran went blank.

"You really are a dimbulb! The aliens aren't after you or your sister, are they? No. They're after your grandfather. He's the one they want. They've already found out they can't get him as long as his family is around, so what would you do in their place? You'd try to separate the family. Right. And we can assume, if everything else about them is true, that they have all sorts of means at their disposal. At least, that's the way I see it."

"Holy Christ," said Fran, as a slow light dawned.

"And one of the talents they might have would be telepathy."

"Sure. Why not?"

That guy in the library! When Fran had gone in he had been ready to work. Then his mind had gradually changed. Had it been changed for him?

"Could be," Eloise agreed. "Even though it's not very flattering to me. Maybe he did use ESP on you."

"But he wasn't an alien, he was just another guy," said Fran.

"Will you *stop*! What says the aliens can't use humans to do their work for them?"

"Holy Christ," Fran said again. "Excuse me. I'll be right back. I'm going to call the hotel."

A few minutes later he was back, looking more distressed than he had when he had left.

"Eloise, I've got to get back to the hotel. It's nine-thirty and nobody has seen Grampa and Palma yet. They haven't checked in. They didn't even pick up the note I left."

"Let's go. I'll go with you. Dancing we can do anytime."

Virgil, footsore and tired, stood on the corner of 59th Street and 3rd Avenue. He was supposed to meet Palma at *The Front Yard* at five. He remembered that place. Palma and her friends had had an all-night dinner here the time she made her high school graduation trip to New York. Must be a pretty good place if it's stayed open all these years.

The late afternoon sun was weary, the air stale. Trucks and buses belched stinking diesel fumes which hung in the stillness like a miasma. Humanity, shoulder to shoulder, crushed along the sidewalks and eddied out into the streets.

Feeling his age, Virgil first checked his watch: four-thirty. He then unrumpled a piece of paper he had taken from his pocket. *The Front Yard . . . 59th between 2nd and 3rd Aves.*, it said. Crumpling the paper back into his pocket, he worked his way along the buildings against the flow of body traffic.

Through the moving jungle of shoulders, he spotted a show going on across the street. A young, bearded juggler, sweating in violet tank shirt and jeans, was hefting six orange balls into the air. The crowd washed around him like a stream around a rock. An occasional quarter dropped into the basket he kept on the ground next to him. From time to time the young man threw his head back and laughed. The traffic noise was so loud that Virgil could not hear the sound of it.

Funny duck. A crazy way to make a living. Virgil figured, though, that New York was filled with funny ducks who had crazy ways to make a living. He wanted to beat the cocktail crowd to *The Front Yard,* so he kept on moving.

He couldn't seem to tear his eyes from the kid as he walked. At one point he seemed to catch the kid's eye. There was a long, unsmiling fixing of stares until a sausage truck with a high back broke it. That kid also had kind of a mean face. For all his goddam smiling and laughing, that was a mean-looking kid.

The Front Yard was cool and dark. A pretty hostess, conscious of her prettiness, led Virgil like a blind man to a table for four in the back.

"Yeah, my granddaughter'll be here any time now," he said.

"Take your time," she smiled like the models on television. "Relax. Have a nice dinner."

It took Virgil's eyes a few minutes to adjust. The place was a large single room; the bar and dining room were divided by a shoulder-high wooden partition. Mounted on the walls were old horse collars, bits, reins, and egg-crate art. Stuff that sure went back before his time. Each table was covered with a red-checkered cloth, in the center of which burned an oversized votive candle.

He smugly noted that he had beaten the cocktail crowd. He ordered a Coke from the waitress.

It felt great to sit. The muscles of his calves relaxed. A surge of warmth flushed through them. Goddam, he sure wasn't the guy he used to be; and Virgil rarely made concessions to his age. No matter what kind of shape he kept himself in, he had to admit he wasn't a kid anymore. Why, back in the days when he had been in the Corps, he would pound the road for twenty, thirty miles with a full pack and never think twice about it. Now he walked twenty or thirty blocks and he was pooped. From his legs, the warmth spread throughout the rest of his body. He longingly tried to remember how his youthful, tireless body had felt.

The Coke arrived. Virgil gulped it. Sitting back to let the coolness take effect, he suddenly felt a ruffle of fear. The warm surges! My God! Just like the afternoon in the League Club! The fear became near-panic, and rose around him like a tide. He clutched the edge of the table with both hands. With his eyes, he fixed some of the objects on the wall, begging them not to disappear.

Where the hell was Palma? It must be near five o'clock. Terror was now squeezing him like a fist. He thought of having one of his spells alone, in a strange city, surrounded by people who didn't know him. What would happen to him? Please, God, don't let it happen. Not here. Please.

The juggler stopped juggling, and he didn't even know why. He just wasn't up for it, man. Even though it was the second busiest time of his day. But when he didn't feel like it, it was time to shitcan it. Rather solemnly he packed away his equipment. A few minutes later he stored his two cheap leather suitcases in the back room of a bar down the street, next to the porno movie. Unhesitatingly, he went back out into the street again.

He was feeling weird: as though a translucent curtain had been drawn between his eyes and the world. He saw different colors. Buildings he knew well seemed to be following the rules of a new kind of geometry. It was like being high. He felt disassociated, disoriented. Under a strange compulsion. He stood wavering in front of the bar like a compass needle waiting for the He stood wavering in front of the bar like a compass needle waiting for the jolt of the pole to give him direction.

Maybe he was flashing back. Had to be. Man, he hadn't dropped a thing for two years now. Ever since that session in the VA hospital.

As though watching a TV screen that had suddenly come to life, a picture formed in his head. Slowly. Discreetly. It was a slender old man with a gray crew cut.

Then the jolt came. The young man tottered down the street toward 3rd Avenue as though jerked by a puppeteer's strings. The picture in his head of the old man became clearer. Like a drunk he bumped his way through the crowd.

He halted in front of *The Front Yard*. He knew the man he was seeking was inside, but he didn't know what he was supposed to do with him. The compulsion said he would talk, would tell the old man something.

Man, the juggler thought, that's a pretty far-out compulsion. It doesn't seem to know I'm a deaf-mute.

Virgil continued to clutch the table, and continued to sink. The warmth that had begun in his legs had spread until, at last, it engulfed his whole body. Furiously, he searched the faces entering the door. Where in the name of Sweet Jesus was Palma?

Minutes passed and nothing happened but the warmth. He noticed that the two young women sitting at the table next to him were looking. With conscious exertion he reached for his Coke.

"Are you all right, Sir?" one of them asked, leaning toward his table.

"Yeah. I'm fine. Thanks."

The young women chatted with him for a few minutes, then returned to their own conversation.

The juggler pushed through the door. There were three or four parties ahead of him waiting to be shown to a table. The juggler stood behind them, not sure what to do. He didn't need a table. What he needed was to just walk up to the old man. His compulsion told him he would then know what to do.

Palma was jittery in the back seat of a cab that was not moving.

"Can't we do something? It's quarter after five already. I'm supposed to meet my grandfather, and he'll be worried to death about me," she said.

"Sorry, lady. I can't do nothing about this traffic. People are going home from work," the driver said, his voice a tone less than gentle castigation.

She sat back and tried to relax, but she had never been known for her patience. The cab was jammed in among a mass of unmoving, honking, screeching vehicles. Maddeningly, they had all come to a dead stop. Had they been closer to 59th Street, she would have gotten out and walked. She felt herself in a trap.

The driver contributed to her frantic impatience by looking so damned unconcerned. And his manners sure left a little to be desired. His tone of voice had been surly. Then bitterly she thought, he wouldn't talk to me like that if I were younger and prettier. He would be fawning all over me.

The bitterness turned to gall. As usual, here she was distressed over Gramps. Hurrying. Rushing. To do something for him. The story of her life. Why wasn't she free to have the evening to herself? Why was it her responsibility to wait on him hand and foot? She could have browsed through the stores until they closed. She might have had a quiet dinner in one of the lovely little places she had seen. Remembering the handsome young men she had seen, she thought she might have met one of them in the restaurant. They might have gone to the theater together. Some of them must be unattached. Maybe they could have gone out for cocktails afterward.

Oh, no. There was always Gramps to look after. It was always *she* who had to do it. Bet your life they wouldn't see Franny for the rest of the evening, probably the rest of the night. Bet your life *he* won't spend tonight alone, worrying about the old man.

She found it easier to relax, thinking these thoughts. "Don't worry. There's no rush," she said to the driver.

Virgil knew, right there and then, that he couldn't wait any longer for Palma. He had to get out of the cocktail lounge right now. The symptoms were getting stronger. The warmth had passed. Again he was feeling the ghost flesh. Again, the tightening sensation around his neck. Again, the darting perceptions within his peripheral vision.

He looked around for the waitress. She was lost somewhere in the laughing crowd. How that laughter had become a hideous counterpoint! He took two dollars from his pocket, folded them, and placed them under his coke glass. He had just started to rise when he became aware of the bearded young man standing at his table, staring at him. Christ, it was that juggler with the mean face. Even *The Front Yard*'s charitable lighting couldn't soften it. At the moment Virgil saw him, that mean face seemed to be casting over with another expression. One that Virgil couldn't easily interpret. Not in his present state of mind.

"What the hell do you want?" Virgil growled.

The juggler continued to stare. He carried pen and pad—a cheap, handsized, ring binder notebook, on which he had intended to write his conversation, but his hands were frozen.

The images in Virgil's peripheral vision were beginning to crowd him. He felt as though his face had turned fluid.

So it seemed to the juggler. His ears and tongue being useless, he absorbed some frightful impact from the old man through his eyes, the only sensory channel open to him. He knew now what he was supposed to do. His compulsion told him he was supposed to take the old man—someplace. In the moment of confrontation, another voice, perhaps an instinct, something deeper and more primal, had struck him as motionless as a statue. There was something wrong with the old man, something of such horror that it went beyond definition.

Virgil stood, his body flushed with the power of his bygone years. He suddenly hated the guy who faced him.

"Look. Buddy," he said, "you better move your ass while you're altogether. This is the only time I'm telling you."

The young man was now obviously frightened out of his wits. Virgil could see that. Instinctively, the young man took two steps backward into the mob of jostlers. He hurriedly scribbled into his pad. He tossed the page onto the table, then turned and fled.

Virgil looked after him for a moment. He picked up the piece of paper. Through his wavering, confused vision he could barely make out the one word that had been written so quickly as to be almost illegible,

"L E P E R!"

Chapter 10

"What the hell do you mean, 'He's just gone'? Where the hell is he?" Fran said with heavy fear.

"I mean he was supposed to meet me for dinner. He got there before me and he left. That's all."

Fran and his sister faced each other across the table of a booth in the coffee shop of their hotel. Eloise sat next to Fran. Palma, sitting alone, felt she was somehow on trial.

"Well, Jesus Christ, Palmie, you must have some idea where he is."

Palma shook her head. "We had lunch together. Then we split up. I wanted to go to Bloomingdale's and some of the other stores, and he didn't want to come. So we agreed to meet at *The Front Yard* at five o'clock. I asked the hostess if she'd seen him and she said she had but that he had left a little while before I got there. That's all I know."

Fran exhaled audibly. "But you know we're in New

York. You just let him walk away so you could go to the stores?"

"Well, I'm *sorry*," Palma almost shouted. "You didn't seem to be worrying yourself to death about him. Here it is ten-thirty and you just showed up." She looked poisonously at Eloise. "Now you're all full of criticism about me. It isn't fair."

"I told you I was doing research."

Palma's eyes this time rested on the mounds beneath Eloise's blouse.

"Sure you were," she said.

"Palma," Eloise said softly, "did he say anything to you before you separated? Does he have any favorite places in New York? Places he might go to?"

Palma shook her head. "I don't think so. He never comes to New York. He just hangs around the League Club back home. I wouldn't be surprised though if he was off somewhere getting himself as drunk as a pig."

"Maybe we'd better call the police," Fran said.

"I don't think it would do much good," Eloise said. "Your grandfather would have to be missing for twenty-four hours before they would even file a report on him. We might go back and check the restaurant again. That would be as good a place as any to start. Get some dimes before we go. We'll call the hospitals."

It took them until eleven-fifteen to find out that Virgil was not in anybody's emergency ward. By the time they got back to *The Front Yard,* the movies were letting out. The restaurant was packed. And they got no more information from the hostess than Palma had.

They stood outside the door, and the night oozed around them. No one had the courage to say, "What do we do now?" Especially Fran. In the cab, coming crosstown, it had struck him how ineffectual he was compared to Eloise. She always seemed to know the next logical step. Maybe he was out of his turf. Or out of his depth. Maybe he was too close to this situation: like the doctor who won't operate on his own family.

The three drifted down toward 2nd Avenue, not speaking, not communicating at all, and Fran, at least, sunken in a morass of defeat. Where *was* Grampa? Where would he even begin looking for him? In Watertown it would have been bad enough, but here in New York . . . Did he leave the restaurant alone? Had he simply wandered off to some old hangouts? No chance; not when he was supposed to have met Palma. Eloise was right. The aliens had tracked them to New York, and had cut out Grampa. Goddammit! He had made things easy for them with his stupidity!

Seven and a half million people, and he was trying to find one single man. The needle in a haystack was a simple project by comparison. Fran was stunned with the kind of frustration that brings tears to the eyes.

They passed the darkened end of a building that opened into a back parking yard.

"Hey, Mister," a raspy voice said, "can you spare a little money? My friend here," he indicated another derelict propped against the wall deep in shadow, "ain't in such good shape. He needs a doctor. I want to get him to the hospital. I sure could use whatever you could see your way clear to spare."

Fran shook his head, barely looking at the wino. He and Eloise continued walking without breaking stride.

Palma, new to the scene, lagged behind, touched by the old man's story, was indecisive about slipping the old guy a dollar. She looked at his feet. She was appalled by the battered shoes he wore, and the sockless ankles as thick and discolored as white sausages. She looked from his feet to his companion's. Only the feet and the lower part of his legs were visible from the shadows.

"Franny!"

She screamed so loudly that the old wino who had approached them nearly jumped out of his clothes!

*   *   *

The smiles by Virgil's bed wouldn't stop, touched as they were with the hysteria of relief. Virgil was awake. He was lying on top of the covers. Fran, Palma, Eloise, and the old wino, whose name was Matthew Remme, sat around him sipping the coffee room service had delivered.

Virgil was okay. That was the important thing. Once again he had returned from teetering on the brink of a cosmic abyss. The same dumb luck that had allowed him to slip out of their grasps had brought him back: reason enough to smile.

Then, too, there was the comic routine of their confronting the stuffed shirt of a night clerk in the lobby as they supported an almost unconscious Virgil, dragging a wino in tow.

"I guess I owe you," Virgil said to Matthew.

"Naw. It wasn't nothing," he answered, embarrassed, very conscious of his appearance around these people, and very conscious, too, that his original motives had not been the loftiest.

"What in the hell happened? I remember walking out of the restaurant and walking down the street, then—nothing else."

By asking, Virgil signaled that he was back to being himself again. On first awakening, he had run through the same trauma he had the night on the back porch. This time he was relieved to discover he had no wounds. He had told the others nothing of the experience he had had.

"You were saved by the oldest cliche in the world, Grampa," Fran smiled. "You know what they say about New York: 'You could drop dead on the street and people would step right over you.' That's exactly what happened to you. You got about halfway down the street and passed out. People just stepped over you until Matthew found you and moved you down to his—uh—hangout. You sat there until Eloise and Palma and I walked by. Palma spotted you by your shoes."

"You took care of me?" Virgil said to Matthew.

"Sure thing," Matthew said.

"I really *do* owe you. I might have been in a bad way without you."

"No big thing," Matthew said from a tiny voice box.

"Things have a way of working out," Fran said to the old wino, knowing that his original intention was simply to use Virgil as a gimmick for collecting a few sympathy bucks.

Fran stood up. Matthew leaped up as though he were ready to dash for the door.

"Look here. This is a family affair, and family things are very important. You don't mind, I'm on my way."

Fran saw him to the door through a chorus of "good-byes" and "thank yous." He slipped the wide-eyed derelict two twenty-dollar bills.

"Why, thanks a million. Thanks a million."

Soon after, Fran took Eloise to a cab downstairs. She refused to let him see her home.

"Save your chivalrous gestures for when I may really need them. Fran, please call me tomorrow. Maybe we can have lunch—the four of us, I mean."

"We'll be leaving tomorrow night."

"Call me anyhow. We'll think of something," she said, as Fran closed the cab door.

When Fran got back to the room, Virgil was alone. He had changed into his pajamas. He sat on the edge of his bed, his elbows resting on his knees: his "thinking" position.

"Palmie's gone to bed," Virgil said. "The door's unlocked between rooms. When we sack in, we can crack the door open."

Fran slouched against the window sill, wondering at his grandfather's sudden caution. The lights of New Jersey glittered over his shoulder.

There was a moment of silence.

"Looks like we lucked out tonight, don't it?" Virgil said.

"I guess we did. You're lucky you didn't wander out into the street and get yourself killed."

"I'm a whole lot luckier than that. I ain't told anybody the whole thing yet, what with Palmie and that girl being here," Virgil said.

Fran's throat became dry. "You mean there was more than just a spell?"

"You bet your sweet hind end there was," Virgil said, and rolled into the story about the juggler. As he finished up, he uncurled a piece of paper he had taken from his pocket.

" 'Leper!' " Fran said. "What does that mean?"

"I think you know."

"I think I do, too," the young man said. "I think it means the aliens have found us. Eloise said they would. I was kind of hoping she was wrong."

"I got some more ideas of my own, but you tell me: What do you think?" Virgil asked.

"I guess it means the aliens were afraid to make an appearance in their natural forms, now they're using humans to do their dirty business."

"That's about the way I figure it, Franny. What about that note? What do you think of it?" Virgil said.

"That bugs me. Why would that guy write a note?"

"That ain't the point. Not yet, it ain't. Don't it kind of look like them spacemen were right about me having some kind of disease? I mean, here's this guy who's under the control of these spacemen. So it figures he thinks like them, you know, like a little bit of them is inside him. He gets one look at me and right away he sees something that nobody else can see. He gets so scared he almost jumps out of his skin. You should have seen it. Maybe I really do have a disease. Maybe it's as bad as them spacemen said. Maybe it *is* a plague."

Fran lit one cigarette and gave it to his grandfather. He lit another for himself.

"I don't know, Grampa. I still wonder why this juggler, who was so scared, would take the time to write a note. Why wouldn't he just say something and then split?"

"You think the aliens put him up to it?" Virgil asked.

"It could have been some kind of warning."

"Look here, if I really do have some kind of a bug, maybe I ought to let these fellows do their cure on me."

"No way. Absolutely not. Tomorrow morning we pick up your passports and we take off."

"I told you before," Virgil said, "we can't go on running forever. Dammit, Franny, it ain't that I don't appreciate what you're doing, but if these space guys can find us in New York, they can sure as hell find us in Dublin, or London, or Paris. This 'sickness' has something to do with the spells, sure as God made little green apples.

"You and Palmie want to take me over so I can see all the old places again. You know better'n I do those old places ain't there anymore. You can't get to them with a jet. Well maybe it's a disease, I don't know what it is, but *I* got a way to get to them. First time I had a 'spell' I went to St. Denis. This last time, I was walking on the highway going to Mt. Blanc. I heard all the big words you and the doctor in Boston were using. Like ESP and teleportation and all that jazz. Bet your ass though, I get there because of this sickness. That's what the juggler saw: the sickness in my head.

"Franny, we got to stop running—and deal with these guys. If I'm such a big threat to the world, you know what they're going to do next time. They going to try to kill me. I'd be lying if I said it don't matter to me. Suppose they kill you and Palmie in the process? I ain't having none of that."

Fran pulled a chair up in front of his grandfather. In a rare gesture of intimacy, he took the old man's hand in his.

"I know what you're saying, Grampa. How do you think I feel? If I thought for a minute those aliens were harmless, don't you think I'd go along with their 'deprograming'? You've been near them. Christ, nearer than I've been. You've felt the hate that emanates from them. It comes at you in shock waves. Can you really believe people like that are harmless?

"Eloise has read about as much on UFOs as anyone you're likely to find. And by her own admission she knows practically nothing. That's what we're up against, Grampa; the unknown. She's given me some things to think about. Now you think about them, too. You're a guy who doesn't scare too easily.

"These people, or whatever they are, are as superior to us as we are, say, to a bunch of carrots. Suppose, for Christ's sake, that's the way they think of us? Even when they talk to us, they use words and concepts that only *approximate* our words and concepts. Suppose you had a carrot in your garden, and it became 'diseased.' What would you do with it? How would you 'cure' it? See what I mean?"

"I see," said Virgil, "but I ain't seen them kill anybody yet."

"No. Not yet. But you yourself said what their next move might be. I think Eloise is right. I think they haven't killed anyone yet because you are the only 'diseased carrot.'"

He squeezed Virgil's hand, and continued. "Don't you know how desperate we are? We came to New York thinking we had given them the slip. Now we find they're all around us and they can get at us anytime they want. Christ, all our running didn't even mess their hair. They've also proved they got the power to climb inside people's heads. I'll tell you about it later, but they even got inside my head over in the public library.

"I don't know where these 'spells' of yours are leading, Grampa. A couple of days ago I was worried to death about them. I know now we're up against something so big I can't even get enough of a handle on it to worry.

"All we can do is keep running until we find the right place and the right time for a confrontation."

Fran and Virgil disengaged their hands.

"Aw, I guess you're right," the old man said. "Maybe we'll give them the slip when we get overseas. But remember when you were talking about how them aliens think about people? You said people were like carrots in a garden. That's funny. I wonder why you said that."

Fran laughed. "Jesus Christ. You're beginning to sound like a psychiatrist—analyzing everything."

Next morning the hotel lobby was a jumble. Knots of people eddied around mounds of piled luggage. The line in front of the cashier's window waved credit cards, counted money, jostled itself, all in its effort to become former guests.

Fran, Palma, and Virgil threaded their way through the lobby. The two men looked intently at the faces around them, wondering what aliens might be observing them through strange eyes.

They took their bags to the East Side Airline Terminal and had them shipped to *Aer Lingus* at Kennedy International. Fran had allowed Palma to pick the airline. She had chosen the Irish Airlines. "It'll be like starting our vacation early," she had said.

They then battled the commute-hour traffic back to Rockefeller Center to pick up the passports.

"How little they are! Look!" said Palma. "I thought they were bigger than this."

"This color picture ain't bad," Virgil said. "Sure better than a lot of them Marine Corps ID pictures I had."

"Don't talk to me about pictures, Gramps. Mine

100

makes me look awful. I look like somebody's great-grandmother."

"Let's get some breakfast. All this running around first thing in the morning has made me hungrier'n hell," Virgil said.

"We might as well," Palma said. "It's only a little after ten o'clock, and our plane doesn't leave until eleven tonight."

Crammed into a tiny table in a 42nd Street doughnut shop, Virgil and Palma bantered about the upcoming flight like a couple of kids. Silent, Fran mentally kicked around what his grandfather had said to him the previous night about ". . . a carrot in a garden."

It had seemed innocent to Fran at the time he had said it. It still did. What significance had Virgil seen in it? After all, Fran had just been making a simple analogy. Who knows? Maybe the old guy *could* see something he couldn't see. The juggler Virgil had told him about had obviously come under the influence of the aliens and had been able to detect the "plague" in Virgil. Since the spells that Virgil was having were also connected with the aliens, maybe Virgil, too, could sense something.

But what?

It amazed Fran that his sister and his grandfather could be so bright. Perhaps the rejuvenating power of morning had dimmed the terrors of the night before. But not for him. The dangers he sensed were still as real. The city seemed like a jungle. Behind every building and tree and bush there crouched an enemy. They had a whole day to kill. How could they do it and not fall into alien hands?

The remainder of the morning was chewed up going to stores, watching Palma act like Dorothy in Oz. They lunched with Eloise at a criminally expensive French restaurant on 53rd Street. Then they waited.

The sun, in due course, moved westward toward New

101

Jersey. Shadows became warm pie slices angling down from saber sharp buildings. They filled subway grates. They turned the streets into checkerboards.

At six, they met Eloise for dinner. That's when she dropped her bombshell.

"That's right," she said in response to Fran's numb expression, "I'm going with you. I talked it over with Lynk. He thinks it's a great idea. So now the guy who used to chase stories *is* the story."

"You told Lynk everything?" Fran asked.

"Fran, he's a good friend. So am I. You trusted me. Why do you find it so hard to trust him?" Eloise said.

"Because I know him. I know how he thinks. He must think I'm out of my tree."

"Do you think he'd be sending me over to Europe with you if he thought you were out of your tree?"

"He might," Fran said. "You're right: he's a friend. He might have sent you along to keep me from injuring myself. I'm an employee, too. Maybe it's part of the fringe benefits."

"Fran, you're just too close. This is a story. A real, honest-to-goodness story. If it were happening to anybody else, you could see it. And what a story. It has no corners or edges. It has nothing but sides that keep shifting around."

"But . . ." Fran began.

"Something's happening to you and your family that may be beyond anything humans have ever had to deal with before. It may impact on all our cosmological theories. Think about that. If you were Lynk, you'd do the same thing."

"If all else fails, it's a hell of a human interest story. *Newsman Pursued By Flying Saucers!*" said Fran.

"I can see how you feel," Eloise continued. "Lots of people before you haven't wanted to have their professional reputations associated with UFOs. Times are changing. UFOs are getting to be like the theories of life after death. The only thing everybody can agree on is that there's more to them than meets the eye."

"You're making us sound pretty important," Virgil said.

Eloise smiled.

Palma, used to being the only woman, held Eloise silently, in an undecipherable stare.

"Will you be coming with us tonight?" Fran asked.

"Oh, no. I can't get away that soon. I still have some loose ends. I'll meet you in Ireland."

The conversation between Fran and Eloise barely washed over Virgil. He dropped a question here and there to let them know he hadn't drifted away, although, in truth, he had. By imperceptible degrees a dissociation had insinuated itself between him and the world. A mist seemed to have risen up around him. It was similar to the sensation he had had that afternoon in the League Club, just before the spell started. And again in the restaurant last night. Only this time he felt as though he was on the verge of some significant enlightenment. As though one more step would take him from the darkness into the light. Those other times, the changes he had noticed about himself had been physical, now it was mental. Spiritual, perhaps.

If he were alone with Fran he might talk about it. If he could find words. It was a new sensation. An hour ago he was cautious and afraid, as Fran was. Now he wanted to tell his grandson that there really was no danger.

This new light he expected to walk in would be more like a new life. Life, with all its simplicity and unthinking vigor. It was youth. It was health. It was an exhilaration for old Virgil. It would be a revisit to paradise.

Virgil had learned to bow under the weight of age. That weight being the proximity of death. Day by day, the aging process consists of accustoming yourself to the inevitability. Virgil had done that. He had gone from thinking of death as a horror. To thinking of it as a void. To finally, thinking of it like the trips to the dentist's office he had taken as a kid that had turned out to be not as bad as he had thought.

Just now, sitting at this table, feeling a regenerated strength within him, Virgil knew with unshakable certainty, that he would never die. He had somehow been deflected. He would continue to rise and fall through untold centuries, like the rejuvenations of spring.

And it would not be life as an old man. It would come complete with vigor, with youth, and with a perpetually renewing sense of wonder.

Virgil felt so excited that he had to get up and move around.

"Excuse me, people," he said. "I gotta go see a man about a horse."

"Down the hallway there. And through the door. See it?" Fran directed, smiling.

Virgil found himself at the base of a set of old wooden stairs. The stairs and the passageway were so unfinished, it made the restaurant look like the facade of a Hollywood set.

He stood for a moment, wondering what he should do. Finally, of course, he headed for the lavatory. Next to the lavatory door, however, was another door, cracked ajar, that looked as though it might be a broom closet. Out of curiosity, he pushed the door open. The light was on. It was the maintenance room. Large boxes of paper towels and toilet paper lined the left-hand wall. Two barrels of disinfectant soap, the other. The odor of disinfectant was almost overpowering. Virgil stepped inside.

Frighteningly, the door closed behind him. Virgil snapped his hand back and tried the knob. He exhaled with relief to find that it was still open.

"Come in, Mr. McCauley."

Even in his euphoria, Virgil shuddered at the sound of the hideous buzzing voice he hadn't heard since that night in his bedroom. The single overhead bulb cast a thick shadow from the piled boxes to the corner behind them. The voice came from that block of shadow.

"Time is getting short. As you see, it is impossible for you to escape. You must accept our assistance. Again permit me to assure you that you will not be harmed in any way."

Virgil stiffened.

"How'd you get in here?"

No answer.

"You guys really are from a flying saucer, ain't you?" Virgil asked.

Again silence.

"My grandson's been doing some reading about you people. He says nobody's ever talked to you before? That true?"

"There have been many conversations," the voice buzzed.

"Yeah? Then how come nobody knows about them?"

"There is forgetfulness," the alien said.

"Funny thing," Virgil said after a moment. "I thought I'd be scared as hell if I ever met you guys again. Here we are, and I'm feeling pretty cool about it."

"You are not the same being you were a few days ago."

"Maybe not. But that don't mean I'm going with you anymore'n I ever would," Virgil said.

"I'm afraid you must. There can be no more delay. Your—ah—illness is progressing."

"*Must,* nothing. I don't have to do nothing I don't want to do. I'm going to tell you how things stand. Last time I wouldn't go with you because I was scared. This time it's different. I'm sure as hell not the same guy I was a couple of days ago.

"You guys, or this disease, or something, changed

105

me. And I like it. Only instead of being like a disease, it's like you gave me a present. I ain't giving it up."

The alien seemed to select his words carefully.

"Accurate. Very accurate, Mr. McCauley. The gift, if you choose to call it that, was given to you in the pine forest near your home the day you thought you were having a heart attack. I can understand why you can consider it a gift. I can understand why you are loathe to give it up. We had hoped it wouldn't go this far. Unfortunately, you do not understand the nature of the gift. It is the 'plague' we spoke of. It was given to you by accident. It is a gift that will kill you. Perhaps, as it runs its course, it will kill your entire race."

"Well, that's as it may be. All's I know is I ain't giving it up. I'm different. I'm young again. I'm strong. Couple of days ago I was a doddering old codger. How can you ask me to give it up?" said Virgil.

"There is no way for you to see the seriousness of the situation. Even the words you are speaking are part of your impending destruction. The moment of dissolution is approaching quickly.

"Mr. McCauley, you *are* an old man, by your race's physiological life term. It is proper that you be so. At least until things—change. Yes, you are young. You are strong. But these characteristics are not proper for a person who has lived your number of years. It runs counter to the very nature of your construction. The cycle of your race's life and death has been defined. At this moment there is nothing in your makeup which will permit you to survive stepping outside those limitations.

"Come to me. Touch me. Return in peace to the race of which you are a member."

Virgil stood.

After a minute of waiting the figure stepped out from the shadow. The light overhead was merciless to it. When Virgil saw it, he flinched.

It was not the black-clad figure that had visited his

106

bedroom. It was the juggler. It was the juggler's body, at least. Except for the essence of the alien that had taken possession of it, the body was dead. It looked as though it had been for a number of hours. The eyes were sunken back into deep sockets. The flesh of the face hung in folds. The clothes were disheveled. The limbs beneath them jerked unnaturally to attain motion. The figure, a mere husk containing an alien intelligence stretched out a lifeless, putrescent hand!

Virgil ducked to the left, slamming his shoulder into the pile of tissue boxes. The top box became dislodged. In a single, athletic movement, he pivoted to the left, wedged his hand behind the box, and shoved it forward.

With a squidging plop, it struck the noisome figure, pinning him against the far wall.

The old man fled into the hallway, down the stairs. He rushed past a well-dressed young man climbing the stairs. The young man stopped, looked over his shoulder.

Crazy old coot, he thought.

"Hi, Gramps," Palma said as Virgil took his seat at the table.

Apparently he looked normal enough, unruffled by his run-in with that creature upstairs. At least, nobody said anything.

Fran and Eloise were making plans.

"Oh, we won't be living in Dublin. We're staying with Darren Gilroy. He's got a big, old converted Georgian place up in County Mayo. Lots of fresh air. Lots of quiet. He'll be meeting us at the airport in Shannon."

"Darren Gilroy? Not *the* Darren Gilroy, of International News Bureau fame?" Eloise said.

"None other: star of stage, screen, and facsimile machine."

"I haven't seen him in years. Is he still head of the Dublin bureau, or did he drop off into the Irish Sea?"

"He still is. He's a lot more than that to us, though. He's a hometown boy. I don't remember a time when I

107

didn't know him. He lived right down the street from us. He's about five years older than Palma. That's about right, isn't it?"

Palma nodded, smiling.

Fran continued. "Christ, he's had a crush on Palma since she was about seven. He was in fifth grade when she started school. He was the one who took her by the hand for her first day in kindergarten."

"This is marvelous! Learning something about Darren Gilroy. He's such a clam. You'd never find out anything talking to him. I first met him in London when I was on my way over to Bonn. After an evening with him, I used to have this recurring nightmare of having to interview him."

"I guess my father was indirectly responsible for getting him in this business. Dad used to work in a print shop. Every day during the summers when Darren was out of school, he used to hang around just to watch the presses work. When he started high school, Dad got him a job in the plant as assistant to the assistant, or something, you know?

"When Dad died, Darren was in BU, Boston University. I think he took it as hard as I did.

"Bet you never knew Darren was the guy who got me in International News. I guess it was his way of repaying a debt to Dad."

"He's quite a lad," Virgil said. "Quiet-like. A thinker."

Palma laughed.

Eloise looked at her, but Palma didn't elaborate.

" 'A thinker.' " Fran laughed. "Lazy, you mean. He's got to be the most laid-back guy on the whole continent of Europe!"

"Don't misunderstand. I liked Darren. He's really a nice guy. But he was so shy you could never get him to take you anywhere. He never wanted to go any place or do anything. All he wanted to do was hang out. A date with him was deadly!" Palma said.

"In a lot of ways I admire the guy. The only things in

108

the world he gives a damn about are hunting, fishing, and reading. And he expends all his energies doing them. He doesn't just dream. You know, he should have Lynk's job today," Fran announced.

"He did a great job in the Middle East during the Lebanese Christian–Moslem War. He got stuff back nobody else could touch. He was really a guy on the way up. They loved him in New York. When he found out he was the Golden Boy, you know what he did? He used all his clout to get himself the berth in Dublin, where absolutely nothing happens. When things started happening in Ulster, damned if he didn't get the company to hire a couple of young kids to cover the stories. He sits in Dublin and edits.

"The rest of his time he spends out in that estate of his sloshing through the marshes. He's such a fixture in those little hunting and fishing towns the Irish have a name for him: Paddy The Yank, they call him."

As they finished talking and paid the bill with an American Express card, none of them saw the Latin-looking maintenance man step from the rest room entrance, shaken and white. Nor did they see the maitre d' follow him upstairs a little later. They were halfway to the airport when the police arrived.

Chapter 11

Dawn moved like a ground fog out of Europe, footlighting the curtain of sky up ahead, rolling across the surface of the Atlantic, turning it heavy, mercury gray. The Pan Am 747 breathed easy on its second wind. The high stars remained icy pinpoints in the still, black bowl of the sky. Shannon, Ireland, was slightly more than an hour away. Soon the lights would go on in the passenger cabin; the flight attendants would be serving coffee and sticky buns.

Virgil, Palma, and Fran, sat side by side in the three-to-a-row seats.

When they boarded at Kennedy, Fran had said, "Here, Grampa, take the window."

"Not me. I'd as soon sit an the aisle and watch the girls."

Fran had given up trying to follow Virgil's hourly mood changes. Respecting what he believed to be his grandfather's first flight nervousness, he offered it to Palma.

"Thanks a lot, but no thanks. I'm perfectly happy surrounded by the two men in my life," she answered significantly.

Virgil and Palma were as giddy as kids during the first few hours of the flight. They giggled over the earphones. They plugged and unplugged them. They switched the station selector around and around. Fran hadn't the courage to point out that they were both wearing the earphones upside down.

Now—like kids—they were tired. Neither the excitement of the new, nor the stereo, nor the movie had been enough to keep them awake. Virgil bunched his coat around him, and slept a dreamless sleep.

Retrieving her jacket from the overhead rack, Palma squirmed onto her left side, and covered her shoulders with it. She nodded off peacefully remembering the pleasures of the morning's shopping trip. She laughed at what a hillbilly she had become.

In one of the shops, she had tried on a long-sleeved, maroon, silk blouse; floppy in the arms, draped in front. The saleswoman, noticing that Palma had buttoned the blouse clear up to her neck, smiled, as at a child, stepped up to her and unbuttoned the top four buttons. Palma's mouth had dropped open!

"Honey," Fran laughed, "they're supposed to show!"

They had swept through more shops, Gramps grumbling every inch of the way. She walked off with eight new blouses, a dozen scarfs, four skirts, a half-dozen sweaters.

"You'll need the sweaters in Ireland," Fran said.

Aboard the 747, Fran's sleep was much less restful. His seat at full recline, he lay facing away from his sister, his head resting against the bulkhead. His mind was a track around which his thoughts chased each other.

For the first time he seemed to see clearly what he was doing. They were chasing around the world for reasons that *really* only Virgil understood.

And Grampa's moods. He was up one minute and down the next.

It seemed to Fran that he was seeing clearly for the first time. What a fool he had been! Maybe he should have had Gramps checked out by the psychiatric nursing home.

Suddenly, everything seemed absurd to Fran: flying saucers, spacemen, my God!

Then there was Eloise. He found it comforting to think about her. She was no ball of fluff. She was a hardnosed reporter, and she could see something.

Fran nodded off, tossed from one side of his mental scale to the other.

And when he slept he did not notice, through the 747's window, in the last minutes of night, an imperceptibly dull ring of light far off in the distance beyond the wing tip. It followed the plane's trajectory for a few minutes. Then, without warning, it swept upward like a comet in reverse. In a second it disappeared into the milkiness of dawn.

There was a moment's consternation in the cabin over a blip on the radar that shouldn't have been there, and suddenly was not.

Chapter 12

It was seven-thirty when the plane touched down at Shannon. High green grass, flattening like grain in a storm, grew alongside the runway. White wooden sheds containing God knows what kind of complicated scientific equipment reminded Palma of old movies she had seen about bomber bases in England during World War II.

Picking up their luggage was the usual hassle. In addition to which, they had to wait through a long line to have their passports validated. They had no sooner gotten to the main concourse when a voice chimed over the public address system.

"Mr. Francis McCauley. Mr. Francis McCauley.

"Please report to Aer Lingus information desk.

"Please report to Aer Lingus information desk."

Fran was halfway there before the soft brogue finished repeating the call.

"It's a message from Darren," he said as he returned.

"He's not going to be able to meet us until about eight o'clock tonight. He says for us to take a cab to Ryan's Hotel in Limerick. He's got rooms reserved for us. And we'll all have dinner together."

"He's a pretty considerate boy, Darren. He's right on the ball," Virgil said.

"Pretty smart, too. It'll give us a chance to grab a nap before dinner time," Fran said.

"A nap! Are you out of your mind? Here we are in Ireland. Really and truly in Ireland, and you talk about taking a nap! Not me! I want to see everything!" Palma said.

"Dear Sister, stop being such a goddam tourist. Haven't you ever heard of a thing call *jet lag?* You have just traveled three thousand miles in less than five hours. You have gotten practically no restful sleep. The sun may tell you it's eight-thirty, but your body is still operating on New York time. Your body thinks it's three-thirty in the morning. If you don't get some rest now, you're going to pay for it later on. You'll be so tired in a couple of days, you won't be able to enjoy anything," Fran said.

He was still explaining when they got a cab outside. Palma might have continued her protestations but she began gulping in the new sights immediately as the cab pulled out.

"I thought it would be different," she said. "It looks just like the States," obviously disappointed.

The driver leaped to her rescue. "This is an airport, Missus. And airports are the same the world over. If you're not impatient, you'll soon be seeing some sights the likes of which you've never seen in America."

Fran felt a suspicion ripple along his spine. He wondered if he should read double meaning into the driver's words. In the meantime, the driver enchanted Palma.

Oddly enough, after a long breakfast at *Ryan's,* it didn't take much to talk Palma into a nap.

114

"I guess I do feel kind of tired. You may be right about the jet lag. I feel kind of funny. My brother, the smart aleck," she said.

Alone in her room Palma sat on the edge of the bed fighting the urge to lie down. Beyond her white-trimmed, walled-sized window, there was an untended field, in the middle of which stood an umbrella-branched tree. As she thought about it, there was a difference between here and home. The air, for one thing, was cooler and cleaner. At home, at this hour, it would be so warm that she would be napping on top of the covers. Here she felt she might use a sheet or a light blanket.

The tree and the field weren't different. Not really. Yet they seemed to be. They were in Ireland. Perhaps she was seeing them through the stories that Gramps had passed down to them from his father.

When Franny had gone to Europe for the first time, he had written her a letter. He had said that when an American lands in Ireland for the first time—if the American happens to be of Irish parentage—he feels as though he's landing in Fairyland. For so long has he lived with the stories and ballads and poems about "The Old Country," that the solid land begins to lose its reality. Truer words, she thought, were never spoken.

Remembering the letter, she lay back, and in a few minutes was sound asleep.

"Well, Darren, it's damn good to see you again," Virgil said, easing away from his dinner plate, upon which only the merest scraps of roast beef and potatoes remained.

"I'm sorry I couldn't have gotten here sooner," Darren said. "Franny didn't give me a whole lot of warning. I was in Dublin when he told me you were coming over. I had to do some maneuvering to get the office covered. Then I had to shoot over to the house to make sure everything was okay. I haven't spent as much time

115

there this year as I usually do, what with the war in the North blowing hot and cold."

"That's our Franny," Palma said, looking at her brother. "When he decides something has to be done, it has to be done *right now*. You know, if anyone does; he's always been like that. I think it's marvelous of you to put yourself out like this. There aren't too many people you could call up at the last minute who would let you use the house, make all the arrangements, and even come meet you at the airport."

"No kidding, Darren, it really is pretty great," Fran added.

Darren waved away the thanks. "When you said you were looking for a place to spend a couple of quiet days, my place sounded like a natural. Don't tell me you wouldn't have done the same—and more—for me. It's all the quiet you could ever want. Wait'll you see it. Right, Fran?"

The dining room of *Ryan's* was low and long and dark-paneled, with heavy, overhead beams. A turf fire burned smokily in the hearth at the far end. The tables were comfortably spaced. Considering the number of foreigners who stopped in, it was quite un-touristy. Compared to an American restaurant of comparable size, it was quiet.

The tourists were finished eating and leaving for their evening activity. It was eight-thirty, the time when local people came drifting in, alone or in pairs, to sit at a table, have a pint and a smoke.

"I love the way they roll their own cigarettes. Look at the tin cans they carry their tobacco in," Palma whispered.

"As good as I'm feeling right now, we can go anytime," Virgil said.

"For heaven's sake, Gramps, you make Darren sound like a chauffeur," said Palma, giving a private, protective look at Darren. He responded with boyish shyness.

"I never meant it like that at all," Virgil said. "That

woman has a way of twisting things you say. Just like her grandmother."

Darren was a little less than tall, a little more than medium; a little less than stocky, a little more than thin. His straight black hair, the slightest bit salted with gray, fell in a disorganized hodge-podge over his brow, around his collar. He wore a Harris tweed jacket, one of those beautiful pieces of material you can pick up only in the British Isles. His, apparently, had been picked up a long time ago. The collar, cuffs, and elbows, looked as though they were about to give out from exhaustion.

His face was the aspect that told all about him. It was unlined, serene, slowly responsive. When something bothered him, his emotions worked beneath the surface like a current below the smooth surface of a lake.

If his face reflected his insides, it also reflected what he had become as a result of his exposure to the world. In a business that chewed people up, Darren had become, if possible, even more serene than he had ever been.

He knew what people thought of him. In fact, he gladly agreed with them. He owned up to the truth of his laziness after his first two years as a correspondent. The schemes and plots necessary for corporate advancement were simply not for him.

"Time spent doing nothing is never time wasted," he liked to say.

He felt there was nothing at the top that justified the price to get there. If it was laziness to prefer fishing in an Irish lake to dodging bullets in the Negev Desert; if it was laziness to prefer a quiet pub to taking notes at a snoremongering meeting of somebody's parliament, so be it.

"And you're still not married?" Palma asked.

Darren shook his head, again smiling shyly.

"I'm surprised. I should think one of these Irish girls would have snapped you up long before this," she said.

Fran laughed. "Where the hell would he meet an Irish *girl?* Unless they start hanging around in a duck blind, or in the middle of a trout stream, he'll never even see a girl."

"I guess I never thought about it like that," Darren smiled.

"What the hell's the rush?" said Virgil. "My father told me men in the old country never got married until they were forty-five. Damn smart idea as far as I'm concerned. Darren's still got some time to go."

"How about that sister of mine? Twelve hours in Ireland and already she's a matchmaker. Maybe we ought to apply for a license."

"I wasn't matchmaking! I was just curious. I mean, Darren is an attractive man, he has a good job. I'm surprised he's not married. That's all," Palma said.

Darren, ill at ease at being the subject of discussion, signaled the waiter for the bill.

"I guess if you guys are all ready, we can get started," he said.

Darren had a red English Ford. As Virgil and Fran supervised the loading of their gear, Palma hung back with Darren near the lawn.

"I'm really glad you could come," he said.

"It's the most thrilling thing that's ever happened to me," she said.

"Yeah, well, I guess there's a lot to see. Maybe I could show you around—ah—when Franny and Virgil are busy, you know. Maybe have dinner in Dublin and go to the Abby Theater, or something."

"Oh, Darren. That would be beautiful. I'm going to hold you to that. That's a promise. Don't forget."

"Don't worry," he sighed with relief. "I won't. It looks like they're all packed. Maybe we ought to go."

Driving out of Limerick, they followed the near bank of the Shannon Estuary. This time of year, the wind from the water was cool and mild. In winter and

118

spring, it howled like a gale, twisting trees into over-sized bonsais, gouging the dry vegetation, searing human cheeks. The roadway was brightly lit. The countryside was spiked with tall, limber poplars. Among the trees, on secluded roads, stood three-story concrete houses with red and green shutters overlooking high stone walls.

Soon the road narrowed. The lights became dimmer and more widely spaced. The water, too, narrowed. The wild estuary became the fabled, placid River Shannon. Further up, they crossed a steel suspension bridge to the west shore, and headed north for Galway City.

Palma pressed her face to the window, not wanting to miss a moment of the fantasy night. The road narrowed down again. This time to a two-lane black-top. Except for an occasional writhing set of head-lights, illumination ceased to exist. The countryside was so dark, the blackness seemed to rise from the ground like a mist. Both sides of the road were flanked with unending stone walls, to the height of about four feet.

"I feel like I'm traveling in a trench," Virgil said.

Only on the crests could they see beyond the walls to the fields that moved gently back toward stygian mountains. A black wind stirred. The occupants of the car could feel it press against the window.

Galway City was an eruption of light. Palma oooohed and aaaahed as Darren gave them a quick tour of the deserted streets. He took them around a square that wasn't unlike the one in Watertown.

"I guess people always dedicate squares to revolutions," Darren said.

"How long does it take to get used to driving on the wrong side of the road? I'm going crazy watching you," Virgil said. At the Imperial Hotel, a lunching spot for VIPs and on Sundays for families, they swung back to the northbound highway. They passed hillside rows of

119

tall, posh, American-style hotels; to the south they saw intermittent slashes of twinkling water.

"Oh, look, Gramps! Galway Bay! Just like in the song!" Palma crowed.

Darren and Fran, in the front seat, smiled at each other.

Once out of the city, still moving north, an even blacker night slammed down on them. Between Shannon and Galway there had been at least the roadside homes lit up. Now there was nothing. Only darkness. The beam of the headlights seemed feeble and vulnerable, tapping out in front of them like a blind man's cane. The curves became tighter. The bordering walls seemed to close in. The hills grew higher and wilder, brooding, faceless.

The further they traveled the more their joy seemed to seep away. Each felt, in the increasing darkness, in the sudden eerie piping of the wind, that some subtle change had taken place in the atmosphere. Virgil tightened his lips. Palma felt like a little girl terrified of the shadows at the head of the stairs.

"Kind of spooky, huh?" Darren said, noticing the silence in the back seat. "We're in County Mayo now. This is really wild country. It affects you sometimes. Especially at night. Like the Badlands of our Dakotas, or the moors in England."

"By God, you're right Darren. This place gives me a mighty snaky feeling. It's darker'n the inside of my pocket. And listen to that wind blow," said Virgil.

"It seems like something out of a ghost story," Palma said.

"As you can see," Fran said, "rural Ireland isn't big on illumination. The Irish are, in fact, very into ghost stories. I guess if we had to live in this darkness, we'd be into ghost stories too."

Darren picked up. "That wind, Mr. McCauley, is from the sea. We're close to it again. Over there to the left, just beyond the hills."

Suddenly, a magnetic hum boomed in their ears, so loudly that it blotted out thought. The four snapped their heads up, then toward one another; fear, primal and unreasoning, stamped into their faces!

A second later the night exploded with an illumination as bright as a nova! The car's engine died. The car had been going downhill, breaking for a crossroads, when the power had gone. Darren had instinctively slammed down on the brake pedal. And that saved them.

A flashing spear of light, no thicker than the diameter of a pencil, blazed down from somewhere above them, and stabbed into the road in the exact spot where the car would have been had it continued to roll!

There was a roar. And an even more intense flash. A great chunky carpet of asphalt and dirt lifted itself lazily into the air, yawned, and in one, soul-shattering explosion, hurled itself into oblivion!

Where a moment ago there had been solid earth, there was now a maw of space. The car teetered on the edge. Darren's hands and feet worked furiously to extricate the car from the ineluctable abyss. To no avail. The car teetered for another few seconds, then, in slow motion, pitched over into the hole. Shrieks rose from the vehicle that at this moment looked more like a tumbling metal coffin.

The light of a dozen suns overhead faded to a dull glow. An object no more than a hundred feet from the ground, circular in shape, as huge as a low-orbiting moon, moved slowly away, humming contentedly.

The car reached the bottom of the pit and settled on its side. The passenger door, now facing upward like a trap door, squealed open. Inside, moans replaced the shrieks. One by one, Fran, Darren, Palma, and Virgil dragged each other from the single exit.

They scrambled up the wall of their almost grave.

"Quick! Before the gas tank explodes!" Darren bellowed.

Having gained the top, they scuttled to the side of the road and hurled themselves over the wall. They had barely made it a few yards into the field when a bluish-orange fireball whooshed up from the hole!

For a moment, time was held in awed suspension, then Fran yelled.

"Come on! Come on! Let's get together. We'll get lost! This way, come on! If they come looking for us they'll be able to see us like this!"

Fran's commands were hardly necessary. Humans in mortal danger tend by instinct to seek safety in other humans. Darren and Fran flanked Virgil and Palma. With nothing to guide them but their terror they charged into the darkness toward the hills in the distance. They tore themselves on bushes. They battered their feet on sharp rocks. They staggered and reeled and stumbled, but they pushed forward as though being commanded by a giant magnet.

At the far side of the field, the base of a sharp incline, they stopped, having reached the end of their endurance. They breathed in gasping tatters. One by one, they dropped to the ground. Only Virgil seemed unstrained, but the others didn't notice it. As they sat they turned to face the road.

They had gone about three hundred yards. In the distance, they could see the car burning dark orange: a smudged, flickering quiver struggling for life in the darkness.

No one spoke for a while. Only the wind, chilled from the sea, nosed around the midnight landscape. Gradually, their breathing became normal. The sweat on their faces cooled.

More minutes passed. The fire banked. First Fran, then Darren, then Palma, relaxed. Virgil sat rigidly, cross-legged, staring intently, looking fierce.

"What the hell was that?" Darren said, at last. His tone was almost prayerful.

"Look, Darren," Fran said, "I owe you an explana-

122

tion. I should have told you before this. We had our reasons for coming to Ireland, but we didn't know—so help me, God—that we were putting you in any danger."

Fran started to tell Darren everything. A few sentences into the narrative, Virgil suddenly interrupted.

"Shhhhh!!"

The old man was as tense as a bow string. With eyes that shone, he stared off in the direction of the smoking car.

The others fell silent.

For a moment there was only the night. Imperceptibly then, a deep throbbing hum grew in the distance. Fran, Palma, and Darren first looked in the direction of the hum, then to the old man. He made no move.

"It's them, isn't it? They're coming back," Fran whispered.

Virgil didn't answer. He remained entranced.

"They know we weren't killed in the car. They're looking for us, aren't they?" Fran continued.

Before this, beginning with the suddenness of the unexpected attack, the four had been galvanized by the kind of fright necessary to self-preservation: they had been spurred by an act of danger to immediate action. Now the danger was understood, it was expected, it was approaching slowly. Their fright turned to paralytic fear.

"Oh, God! Look!" Palma hissed.

Above the smoldering ruins of Darren's car, a circle of pulsing bluish light appeared, first dimly, then bright and distinctly. It hovered for a moment. It was only three hundred yards away. It seemed to be probing the ground beneath it.

"Holy Christ! They've got us!" Fran breathed.

As the sinister vehicle began to slip toward them, Palma screamed hysterically. Darren threw his arms around her and jerked her to her feet.

"Come on!" he said, "let's get the hell out of here!"

Darren carrying–dragging Palma, Fran stumbling

along beside them, they again crashed through the night. They clutched at the only protection they could find: another stone wall. They rolled over the top and pressed themselves to the ground on the other side. It was then they realized that Virgil wasn't with them.

The humming grew louder. The night around them was turning light. Fran scrambled up the wall.

"Hey, Grampa! Hey, Grampa!" He screamed.

Palma clutched at her brother's clothes. "You can't go back!"

Both Palma and Darren trying to restrain Fran, they struggled to the top of the wall, where, in the pulsing light of the UFO they could see the old man, rigid, unruffled, sitting upright on the grass. The saucer was directly over his head!

Palma screamed!

What happened next neither Fran nor Palma nor Darren could accurately describe, even later, and in that moment they felt a fear that went beyond definition.

The universe seemed to waver. Those lines and forms which are always distinct, suddenly became ambiguous. Darren, who glanced downward for a moment, swore that the wall they were leaning on began to turn invisible. Palma felt the earth under her feet become insubstantial. Fran was stunned almost into shock to see the field turn to a sudden cacophony of flashing, swirling light, multicolored, swarming, shifting, moving. Later, he also thought he saw figures taking form over the prosaic vista in front of him. It was like a double-exposed film. Or even more so, like a cinematic cross-fade, ending one scene, beginning another. The lines he saw might have been those of a street in a small town.

He looked up to the saucer, as did the other two. It too was besieged with the swirling colors. Its outlines began to blur.

The hum rose to the pitch of a scream. The machine reared itself up, then lurched toward the road. Its lights went out. Only an ugly swooshing of air attested to its hasty retreat as it angled upward and rejoined the other cold, alien things in the night sky.

When Fran, Darren, and Palma reached Virgil, he was wide awake. The corners of his lips were turned upward in a cryptic smile.

Chapter 13

*E*loise Courtney landed at Shannon Airport the next morning and she, too, found a message waiting for her. She rented a car and drove like mad to the town of Swineford, in County Mayo. She found Fran, Darren, Palma, and Virgil cooling their heels in the police station.

Two black-uniformed *Garda* escorted her into a spacious room in the rear of the building where they sat around a rough, wooden table drinking tea.

"Ah," said the inspector in charge, "I believe your friend has arrived."

"What happened? You four look as though you've been run through a Mixmaster," she said, breezing over to them.

Eloise hugged Palma.

"Darren, it's good to see you again. We have tons of things to talk about," Eloise said, moving from Palma.

"Nothing much happened. We just had a bit of trouble," Darren said.

"Indeed, they did," the inspector agreed.

The way he said it, it sounded more like a question. She put her arms around Fran. "I'm so glad you're okay," she said.

"We're okay. We had a run-in with the bomb throwers, that's all. We've been filling out some papers."

When Eloise got to Virgil, she was shocked at the changes that had come over him since yesterday. His cheeks were glowing pink and radiant. His eyes were clear. The dewlaps beneath his chin seemed to be tightening. His body, always lean, seemed now more youthfully lithe.

She kissed him on the cheek.

"Things are jim-dandy," he smiled.

"And how was your trip?" the inspector asked Eloise.

"Fine. Good weather," she answered.

"Isn't it a shame that your first day in Ireland has to be spent tending business like this?" He rose from his chair and fingered his cold pipe. "Well, I see no reason for detaining you any longer."

After a last few words at the front door, the inspector watched the Americans walk to the car the rental agency had just delivered. He jotted down the license number. He turned to the main hallway and signaled to a young man who was lounging in a chair next to the sergeant's desk.

"Daly," he called, motioning toward his office.

"You saw our American friends?" Inspector Eamon Cready said to Daly over his shoulder as he dialed the phone. "What do you think of them?"

"Nice enough sorts," the young detective shrugged. "A terrible bit of luck: being bombed the first night."

"Yes. That's true," the older man said. "A nice enough sort, truthful types. I wonder how much of what they told us about their car is the truth?" Cready said.

"Do you doubt them?"

"That's what I'm not sure of. I am, however, a man who asks questions for his daily bread. Everything seems proper enough, but I keep asking myself: what sort of bomb could make the hole we pulled the automobile out of? It was as deep as a well. The sides were straight and smooth. And—did you notice?——there was hardly a grain of dirt to be found that should have been thrown up by the explosion.

"Did you notice that the tar around the rim of the hole—just at the very edge, mind you—was melted? As if by a great heat. I ask you again, and you're a man that has seen his share of bomb craters, what sort of bomb could make a hole like that?"

"Phosphorous, perhaps. Some chemical thing," Daly answered.

"Yes. I've thought of that. Phosphorous would certainly do a bloody job on the tar, but it wouldn't dig a hole that deep."

"Maybe the yah-bos have a new sophisticated bomb."

"I'm hoping not. Because there is a familiarity about some of the signs."

Daly waited for his boss to continue.

"When I was taking a training course in Dublin a year or so back, didn't I see some English Specials give a demonstration of a Laser beam? Now before you even ask, to save me I can't imagine how any of the militants would have come into possession of Laser. It's merely a thought that's working at me.

"Something else. They said they crawled out of the car and rushed into the field behind the east wall. Then, they said, they ran across the field. Does that strike you? First off, that wall was the only place for a bomb thrower to hide. If not there, where? The opposite side was clear ground because of the crossroad. Second, it is not the nature of terrorists—at least our home-grown variety—to toss one bomb, and run. It is much more likely, in such isolated surroundings, for them to finish you off with rifle fire."

While Cready was speaking, he packed and fired his pipe.

"You see?" he continued, "we're getting all questions and no answers. I wonder what the Provos, or whoever they are, are doing this far west. I wonder why they would try to kill four foreigners who have no record of having taken sides, one way or the other, in the Troubles. I can see their going out of their way for the likes of Mountbatten, but not these citizens."

"Are you thinking we're not quite done with them?" Daly asked.

"Would it be too much trouble for you to spend some time following them about?"

"Not at all."

"Good. The Yanks were such charming people, I think we should get to know them better."

It was after six when the four travelers got to Darren's house in County Mayo. The house was a pre-Georgian brick, a mansion left over from the Ascendency days, which no amount of repair could make look new. The brick was no longer bright red; the house seemed to have imperceptibly, over the years, taken on earth color of its surroundings.

The ride from Swinford had been strained and uncomfortable, but they spent a calm night in the old house. And there, Eloise helped Fran explain to Darren what had been happening to Virgil.

"I'm sorry we got you into this mess. We won't think anything wrong if you want to pull out. You have that much coming," Fran said.

"That's a fact, boy," Virgil agreed. Then ominously added, "Things may get a hell of a lot worse."

"I wasn't thinking of pulling out. I'm just glad to know what's going on. I didn't know what to tell those cops. I just kept shaking my head. Whatever you guys said was good enough for me. I was terrified they'd split us up, as cops usually do. If they had questioned us individually, I wouldn't have known what the hell to say."

The others were a little puzzled that Darren could accept the situation as readily as he did.

With Darren's help, they explained last night's incident to Eloise.

But neither Fran nor Palma nor Darren mentioned the thing that was bothering them most: what had brought about that final, apocalyptic instant that had undoubtedly saved their lives, even though it had driven them to the ambiguous border of rationality? During the long silences of the drive, it was this that weighed on them.

Fran could neither control nor could he orient the feeling that the balance had somehow changed; that his grandfather had attained a dimension more comprehensible to the aliens than to his family. The aliens had been a moment from striking them dead when they had been countered by a force equal to their own. Virgil had somehow been responsible.

That night, in the darkened bedroom, Virgil was deviled by the same thoughts. He knew the kids had become aware of the changes in him. He tried to evaluate those changes but each day, it seemed, they altered direction and intensity. At first, to Virgil, it had simply been a matter of youthfulness. What had happened last night that was so new? He tried to recall the incident step by step.

He had been tired when he had heard the hum of the saucer coming back for them. With certainty, he knew the aliens had reached the limit of their patience with the childish game they felt was being played with them. It was almost as though he could read their thoughts.

Knowing this, and knowing the extent of their power, he had been suddenly stricken with paralytic fear. The others panicked, and he was alone. His terror increased.

As the advancing saucer lit up, he was a mouse in the coils of a snake. The slow-moving vehicle seemed to send out before it wave after wave of vibrations that

130

battered his brain like surf battering a rocky shore. The horror grew until, at last, Virgil could no longer endure it. His all-too-human mind deserted him. It withdrew into the safety of its own fantasy.

It imagined itself back in Watertown, a tree-lined street, familiar shapes, among familiar people. Virgil's blank eyes were half open as the saucer closed the final space between them. Through the slits, he saw his delusion weave itself around the saucer, engulfing it. He felt the vibrations climb to the rise of a scream. A great shower of mental sparks finally blotted out the vision. His mind seemed to have climbed deep into his body by the time the kids had come back for him.

Chapter 14

*N*ext morning, breakfast was a lengthy affair. It was very like a council of gloom where each one clung to his chair, fearful of leaving lest something worse happened.

Palma was lightheaded. Perhaps all the traveling had affected her psychologically as well as bodily. There seemed to be so many undercurrents, she could hardly keep them straight. Each one seemed to talk in riddles, trying to hide something from the other. In time, though, she began to discern patterns: Franny, Darren, and Eloise on one side, and Virgil on the other. In her present frame of mind it all seemed fantasy, anyway.

"Well," Fran said, as though he had reached a conclusion, "I guess it's about time we got ourselves pulled together—that is, if we're going to Dublin. Maybe we shouldn't."

Virgil laughed. "The hell you say! We should be there right now."

They all laughed.

"I guess you're right, Mr. McCauley. And it wouldn't be fair to Palma. She's never seen the city before. It might be fun for her."

"I'm glad you said that, Darren," Palma said, "otherwise it would have made me look like a selfish witch. I never have seen Dublin. I don't want to settle in here at Darren's until I've at least had a chance to look at Dublin."

"Look, honey," Fran said. "We're in danger. We have serious things to do."

"Well, you just go ahead and do them. I'll go down by myself. Don't worry about me. I'll be all right. I'm not going to take any foolish chances. You know me better than that," Palma said.

"That's the dumbest thing I ever heard! How the hell are—" Fran began.

"Now, hold it a goddam minute," Virgil interrupted. "Sure we're in danger. And there ain't nobody sitting at this table that's scareder'n I am.

"So far, we been through some bad things, and we done it all together. If this crap had happened to any one of us personally, he'd be soft as a grape right now. This is a scary situation. Christ, I'm surprised the whole bunch of us ain't off our rockers. I'm telling you this: if we ain't nuts, it's because we been going through this together. And, you know, it's like we're strong because we got each other. That's the way it works when you're in combat: if one guy had to do it all by himself, he'd turn around and run like hell, but he gets strength by having the other guys around.

"I think I'd be dead right now if you people weren't around to help me. They coulda just picked me off like nothing. We're safe, or at least we've lasted as long as we have, because we're together.

"Franny, I guess what I'm saying is that Palmie has been one of us. We play this game like she doesn't know what's going on, but she does. She's stuck with us and she's been a good soldier about it. Don't you think we owe her this much? I mean, shit, if she wants to see the city, let's show it to her. Like Darren says, we'll be as well off there as we'll be anyplace. It's important to her, Franny."

Fran looked around the table and realized he was outvoted. With a shrug he indicated it was out of his hands.

"Okay," he said, "if that's what you all want. Palma, I don't mean to be the heavy. I just don't want anybody getting hurt, that's all."

Palma squeezed her brother's hand.

"You know, Grampa," Fran said, "it's just a damn good thing you never decided to take up a career in politics. You're a great spinner of words."

The mood immediately lightened.

Palma was pleased at the way Gramps and Darren had taken her side. Especially Darren. Even though he was an old shoe, it made her feel like a woman. She liked the way he had been doting on her, too. He was still as shy around her as he had always been: he tried to make up in small gestures what he couldn't bring himself to say, opening doors, holding her chair. Strange that she should make him so tongue-tied. He was a man who made his living with words.

It was kind of flattering to be looked after. A week ago, she had been the strength in the family. Virgil had been a tired, old man who needed her as the mainstay of his life. Fran had been away.

Everything had changed since then. This funny illness had happened to Virgil, an illness which had strangely revitalized him. Suddenly her brother had taken over. She was being treated like a little girl. In another way, it was not so flattering. As long as she stayed within the walls of the house in Watertown, she was somebody. Outside, they treated her as though she were lost and helpless. Well, they needn't patronize her too much. Nobody worried for all the years they had left the burden on her.

The visitors stowed some of their gear at Darren's, repacked smaller cases to take to Dublin and early in the afternoon got into the rented car to head for the other side of the country. They drove back to Swinford and then took the highway on to Dublin, where they were checked in at the new Jury's Hotel. Darren had an apartment in the city, but it was too small to accommodate guests.

After a lengthy dinner, they retired for the evening, though Fran and Darren had a few ales in the pub before Darren went back to his flat.

In the morning, the two women and Fran and Virgil met for breakfast, and sat chatting over coffee. Palma was eager to get started seeing the city.

"Since we're not in any hurry, we might as well have some more of this stuff they call coffee," Fran said.

"You can if you want to. I'm going upstairs and getting dressed," Palma said.

"Don't go alone," Fran said.

"Oh, for heaven's sake, I'm not a baby!"

Eloise, having received a significant nod from Fran, stood up. "That's not a bad idea. I'm a mess. I just threw myself together this morning."

Palma and Eloise headed for the elevator.

Upstairs, all the questions that Palma had about the recent changes in her life seemed to evolve around the differences between herself and Eloise.

"Are you in love with Franny?" Palma asked, as each woman put the finishing touches on her attire.

Eloise was standing at the foot of her bed checking the juncture of her skirt and blouse in a full-length mirror on the closet door. She looked at Palma with an undecipherable expression.

"I like him very much. I've known him for ages. He's

the one who broke me into the business. We're good friends."

Palma felt helpless at this answer. Eloise was a different kind of woman. What did she mean by "friends?" It hurt Palma not to be able to communicate. If incomprehensible changes had come into her life, it was natural that she shouldn't be able to talk about them to a man, but Eloise was another woman. Yet a gulf existed between them. Palma wanted to talk to her. To learn, even though Eloise was ten years younger.

Ever since she had left the house in Watertown, Palma felt that she had walked into a new world about which she knew nothing. A whole world, not just the changes that had taken place in her private world. True, she resented this other woman's intrusion. These were the only people to which she, Palma, had any claim. And she hated the ease with which Eloise did it. Palma had taken care of their house and had made a home of it. Franny and Gramps loved her for that. Respected her. She had stature with them. But did they like her as a person? They seemed to hold her at a distance while they went about their business and she went about hers.

Eloise just breezed in and had been immediately accepted by the men: Gramps, Franny, and Darren. She seemed to be one of them, to talk their language, to be interested in the things they were interested in; not only that, but to understand and care. Was Eloise just an individual, or did she represent all the women her age?

In the few hours they had shared the room, Palma had noted the differences between herself and Eloise. Before, Palma had always believed that the difference between any two women was a small matter.

Eloise's wardrobe consisted mainly of suits and chic silk dresses, hers, a mixed bag of skirts and blouses and pants. Eloise's underthings were prettier. Eloise seemed more cavalier about her clothes, but they were more expensive, and once on, hung better, looked more stylish. Whereas Palma expended great effort with her hair, Eloise just ran a comb through hers. Palma, on the other hand, daubed her makeup; Eloise applied hers like an artist working on a canvas, especially the eye makeup.

At bedtime last night, Palma had gone into the bathroom to change into her robe, after which she had carefully applied her cleansing cream. Eloise had splashed some water on her face, shucked out of her clothes, draped them over the back of a chair, and dived into bed stark naked. Palma carried enough cosmetics to fill an overnight bag. Eloise's could fit into her purse.

What was to be learned from these little differences? How could they explain the difference in treatment both women got? Palma knew she would have to look deeper.

She had a job, but Eloise had a career. Certainly that would change anybody's perspective. Palma, however, couldn't see the other side because to her a job had always been just a way to tread water while waiting for Mr. Right to come along. What did Eloise want out of life? If not a man, a home, children? Was business success enough?

Even the words between the two women were a mystery to Palma. Whenever she tried to talk plain old talk it didn't seem to interest Eloise. If the subject was serious, Palma seemed to herself a bundle of cliches, as though she were quoting from a romantic novel.

What was a woman supposed to be these days? What did men expect from them? Whatever the goal women were reaching for, Eloise certainly seemed more successful attaining hers than Palma did.

She wondered, too, if Eloise would feel the same sense of loss if she had failed in her career as Palma had.

"Fran seems to like you quite a lot," Palma said.

"You bring him out of himself, you know. Nobody else but Gramps can do that."

"I feel the same way. Fran's easy to be around. We work well together."

Another flash of anger heated Palma. Yes, you two work well together, she thought. Downstairs, the nod Fran had given Eloise had not been lost on Palma. Work well together, indeed! And she was just another thing they worked on? If nothing else, Palma had learned from Eloise: if you want to do something, you just go right ahead and do it!

Palma made a big number of looking at her nails.

"Have you got an emery board?" Palma asked, innocently.

"I've got a file."

"No. I can't use a file. They're too rough. Oh, wait a minute. Did you notice that little vending machine in the alcove near the elevators? It sells all sorts of things: combs, nail clippers. I'll bet I could get an emery board there!" Palma took her purse and opened it. "Good. I have some Irish change. Don't go away. I'll be right back."

"Gone! Where the hell did she go?" Fran said, rising from his chair.

"I don't know," said Eloise, helpless. "She just slipped out from under me. She said she was going down to the vending machine to get an emery board, and she never came back. After she'd been gone five minutes, I went looking for her. I searched the whole floor and I couldn't find her."

"Oh, shit!" said Fran. "What a time she picks to get clever! Where the hell would she go?"

"Keep your hair on, boy," Virgil said, "she'll be all right. She's just got it in her head she wants to be alone for a while. She's always been like that. She probably grabbed a cab and headed down to the stores. Don't worry about her."

138

Fran turned on his grandfather. "Don't talk like a goddamed idiot," he snapped. "What the hell do you mean, 'don't worry'? Those bastards are not just after you anymore. They're after all of us. Didn't you learn that the other night? I'm worried and I got damn good reason to worry."

Virgil winced at Fran's vitriol. Fran had never used such a tone before.

"Let's get off our tails and search this hotel," Fran continued.

The three of them stalked out into the lobby, a subdued Virgil bringing up the rear.

"Wait a second. Let's be logical about this. If she did go downtown, maybe she left a message for us," Fran said.

"Yes, sir. Here it is," the clerk said.

Fran hurriedly unfolded a Kleenex.

"Jesus Christ!" Fran said, "Let's get to the car."

He handed the note to his grandfather. Scribbled in eyebrow pencil, the message:

Have gone shopping. See you at 4pm. Love. P.

Chapter 15

"*A*re you all right, Miss?"

Palma, with intense effort, tried to clear her head. She felt a gradual subsiding of the weakness in her body, of the grayness behind her eyes. A hollowness in her stomach seemed to be draining the vitality from her. The last time she had felt like this was when she was a little kid going to high Mass to receive communion and she had fasted since the previous night's dinner. She remained propped against the wall, lest her rubbery legs betray her.

"Yes. Thank you. I'm fine now. This is so stupid. I think I was going to faint." What she hoped was a smile turned out to be a lemony grin.

The concerned expression on the man's face gradually melted. He smiled, clear and open.

"Good for you. It's nothing to be ashamed of, I assure you. You *are* coming about. You're getting a bit of color back again."

"I feel much better. You're very kind," Palma said.

"Nonsense. Here, let me hold your packets for a bit. You're American, aren't you?" he said, relieving her of two large paper bags.

"Yes. I'm from Boston. Actually a little town outside of Boston. I guess you could tell from my accent."

"So? John F. Kennedy country, is it?" he laughed. "That won't go against you over here. A marvelous man: John Kennedy. He was American enough for us to love him, and Irish enough for us to hate him. If you stay long enough, get to know the Irish well enough, you'll know what I mean."

"I feel silly spoiling my first shopping trip by fainting," Palma said.

"I might have predicted it. Irish taxes are frightful enough to make anyone faint. I do it myself regularly."

Palma was pulled together enough to be conscious of the man. He stood facing her, rather boldly she thought. His steadying hand rested against the building behind her left shoulder. Around him the stream of other shoppers flowed as though he were a rock. Amused and curious faces. She was not as conscious of the stares as she might have been. The man's presence was overpowering. The arm extended over her shoulder seemed to emanate a penetrating warmth.

He was tall, slightly taller than Darren. His sandy hair was loose and wavy, flowing down over the virile irregularity of a craggy brow. His eyes were brown, set into deep, rugged, Celtic features. His voice was rich. His accent cultured, an inseparable combination of English and Irish. He wore a white shirt, a maroon tie, a gray wool suit. He was about forty.

"Have you thought it might be the change of climate? It affects some people like that."

"Really," Palma said.

"I once spent some time in your Southern California, and I couldn't adjust to the desert air. A bit too dry for a lad who's used to air that carries its own water supply.

Felt as though I were going about with cotton in my mouth."

Palma smiled, hoping she wasn't indicating how much his proximity was disturbing her. She felt she ought to put some distance between them, but she couldn't trust herself to abandon the supporting wall.

"See here," he said, consulting his watch, "it's almost noon. You're still looking a bit peaked. You need a place to relax and have a cup of tea. I know a tea shop half a block from here. It should still be quite empty. Now I want you to forget the social amenities and allow me to take you. Here, take my arm."

Palma hesitated. "I . . . uh. . . ."

"My dear girl," he laughed.

She took his arm, leaning against the strength of his shoulder. The flesh beneath his jacket was firmer than she had expected.

"Actually," he said lightly as they started to walk, "I don't like to think of myself as harmless where beautiful women are concerned, but we *are* in a public place."

Palma laughed. She was charmed. "It's very nice of you to put yourself out like this. You must have someplace to go. I mean, you must have been going somewhere when you saw me."

"I assure you, I was doing nothing more important. After all, I couldn't besmirch Ireland's reputation for hospitality by letting our American visitors drop all over O'Connell Street. Now, could I?"

Relaxed, Palma let the man lead her down a side street.

"I was just thinking," she said. "All this looks familiar to me, and this is the first time I've ever been in Dublin."

"An American friend of mine, a lad from Los Angeles, once told me that every American who visits the British Isles for the first time is stricken with a rather continuous sense of déjà vu. Everything seems familiar. The fact is, you *have* seen it all before. Dozens of

142

times: in the cinema, on telly. Over and over again, until it seems that you have actually been there. Or here, I should say."

The tea shop entrance was something out of a storybook. Inside, a stainless steel steam table flanking the right wall boiled up a cloud of vapor redolent of fine spiced meats and vegetables.

"They're getting ready for luncheon," the man said.

The opposing wall was lined with dark-wood booths, high-backed and snooty. The tables were marble-topped. A counter down toward the front on the left-hand side was loaded with pastries.

Palma let herself be guided to a booth, she on one side of the table, he on the other. He arranged the packages next to himself.

"Oh, it's lovely," Palma exclaimed.

The mingled smells of candy and pastry, baked bread, meat and vegetables, warmed her beautifully.

From an unsmiling waitress he ordered a pot of tea and a plate of cookies. Biscuits, he called them.

"Thank heavens for foreign visitors," the man said. "Sooner or later, you see, they find themselves downtown to places like this. So the management tries to give better service than it would give to the residents. Most tea shops, the ones away from the downtown districts, don't serve at tables at all. If you want anything, you can bloody well get up and get it yourself."

"My name is Palma McCauley," she smiled.

"McCauley? You certainly have the proper credentials. Perhaps you're one of the long lost American cousins we hear so much about."

"What's your name?" she asked.

The phone rang. Fran's hand shot out.

"Hello."

"Hi, honey."

"Palma! For Christ's sake! We're worried to death about you! Where are you? Do you realize it's ten-thirty at night? You were supposed to meet us at four. Where the hell are you?"

His sister's voice was heavy with sensuality.

"I'm fine. You don't know how fine I am."

"For Christ's sake, Palma, where are you? I'll send a cab. Or I'll come get you."

"Save your cab. I'm in heaven, and I intend to stay there," she hummed.

Pause. "Palma. Listen to me. Have you been drinking?"

"Uh huh. A bottle of wine with dinner. And, let's see, three cocktails afterwards."

"Let me send a cab for you," Fran pleaded. "I don't want you out on the streets at this hour. You know it's not safe."

"What makes you think I'm out on the streets? I could be somewhere else, you know. What's more, I'm staying. I just called to tell you not to worry."

"Are you telling me you don't intend to come back to the hotel all night?"

"That's right." Fran could see his sister's grin.

"You're out of your head!"

"That's right. I am. Way out."

"What are you doing? Who are you with?"

"Who I'm with is my business. If you can't figure out what I'm doing, you haven't been around as much as I gave you credit for."

"You can't do that! You're in danger. Christ, Grampa's here, and everybody else. What the hell are they going to think?"

"You're sounding very prudish. What they think is their business," Palma said.

Fran picked his words carefully. "Look, Palma, I know you're a big girl now and all that, but. . . ."

"That's right," she interrupted, "I'm a big girl now. It wouldn't hurt if you'd remember that. I don't need you or Gramps or Darren, and most especially your girl friend, to look after me. I'm thirty-six years old. I'm

144

single. I'm big enough to make my own decisions. Just in case you haven't noticed, other people have."

"Palma. Listen to me. You're going to hate yourself tomorrow."

"Franny, my dear little brother, you're being a prude again. No. You listen to *me*. You've got things going in the wrong direction. It's when I come home, and I'm alone that I hate myself. Don't worry about me. You can tell Gramps anything you like. But I am not coming home tonight. Maybe I'll see you in the morning, maybe I won't. And please, Franny, don't lecture me. I don't have to take that from you."

Palma hung up.

Fran sat on the edge of his bed for a full fifteen seconds, holding the dead phone in his hand before he returned it to the cradle.

He couldn't believe the conversation he had just had. What the hell was happening to his life? Everything seemed to be falling apart: all those things that he used to depend on, as he depended on the rising of the sun. There had been gall in her voice. She had sprayed it at him as though it had been pent-up for years.

Hell, maybe she had it coming, he thought. While he had been living his life, and Grampa had been living out his final years, Palma had been worked into a corner. All her childhood dreams had been stolen from her. Though it was true that she was in danger, what kind of an idiot was he being? What right, in fact, did he have to tell her what to do? He guessed it was the surprise of it all. She had been such a typical spinster that he had pitied her. She had accepted that pity as her lot in life. Now, suddenly, she was standing up and fighting back: against him, against Grampa, against all of life. It was as much of a surprise as the changes that had been taking place in Grampa.

Fran rose. He took his cigarettes from the night table, and went out the door. All the way down the red carpeted hallway to the elevator, he tried to imagine

145

his sister in the arms of a man. He had never even thought of Palma in relation to sex. For her he had always imagined sex would be a matter of marriage, and home, and children. Oh, boy, he thought, and you're supposed to be so sophisticated!

Fran stepped into one of the hotel restaurants, the dark, little, intimate one. When the waiter arrived he ordered tea.

"I believe you're being paged, sir," the waiter said, indicating a table in a dark corner.

Dubliners being late eaters, the room was crowded. It took Fran a minute to make out Eloise's face.

"Oh, yes," Fran said, standing.

"Would you care to be served at the table with the lady?"

"Yes. Thanks." Fran followed the waiter to Eloise's table.

"I'm too tense to sleep," Eloise said. "It was pointless to go to bed. I'm terrified about Palma. So I came down here."

"You can relax then. She just called. She's okay," Fran said, dully.

"Really?"

"Yeah."

"Thank God. Oh, that's great. Where is she?"

"She's out. With a friend." The irony wasn't lost on Eloise.

"Oh? I didn't think she knew anyone in Dublin."

"She doesn't. Evidently Dublin is a great place for meeting people."

"Did she say when she'd be back?"

"Yeah. Tomorrow. Maybe."

Eloise paused for a moment. "Don't worry about her. Things are fine as long as she's all right."

"You can afford to say that. She's not your sister."

"If she were, I'd also remember that she's a woman. She has to get comfort where she can find it."

146

Fran chose to carry the conversation no further.

"I wonder how Grampa and Darren are," he said.

"Still out looking. I feel sorry for poor Mr. McCauley. He's blaming himself for her being gone."

"No. I'm learning it's something she had to do," Fran said.

"And Darren is out of his mind."

Fran allowed himself a smile. "I'm not surprised. He's been carrying a torch for her as big as Miss Liberty's for years now. Palma's the only one who doesn't know it."

"She knows." It was her turn to smile.

"Funny about those two," Fran said, "it's like they've spent their lives out of phase with each other. When they were little kids she considered him an 'older man.' After all, he was in high school. When they finally grew up to each other they dated a little, she was thinking about hearth and home, and he was getting ready to travel around the world. She wouldn't touch a guy who wasn't planning to settle down right away."

"It makes you wonder about her personal feelings, doesn't it?"

"What do you mean?" he asked.

"Only that some women seem to have love and marriage so tangled up in their minds they can't tell one from the other. It must be nice to be able to pick who you're going to fall in love with. If he has this and if he does that, then I will fall madly and uncontrollably in love with him."

"I thought it was like that with all women," Fran grinned.

Eloise did not respond to the grin. She continued evenly, "Not with me. I have my work, and that's my life. But I'm human. I also need love. Having my work makes me invulnerable. I don't have to marry for financial security. I'm free to take love as it comes along."

"As you *need* it."

"As I *find* it."

Fran seemed at a loss.

"Am I shocking you?" Eloise smiled.

"Hell, no. Why would you shock me?" he said, defensively.

"Because I'm just really getting to know you. That makes me think I might shock you. I think you know where the conversation is going. And I think you're having trouble handling it."

Fran was silent.

"I'll tell you something else about me, if you want to hear it. I'm not a person who can feel one emotion at a time. I can't build fences around them. One has a way of leading to another.

"When I first met you, you were my mentor. You were the experienced older man who could solve all my problems for me. Who had the answer to all my questions. You don't know what that does to a woman's insides."

Fran spoke while she took a sip of tea. "Not just women. I guess I feel that way about my grandfather. He's been my idol all my life."

"Maybe you know the feeling. But it's different between a man and a woman."

She lifted the cup again, and with dramatic effect, looked at Fran over the rim. "Do you know you could have had me any time you wanted me, those two years in Bonn?"

"I—uh—never thought. . . . It's not that I. . . ."

"Don't apologize. I know what you're saying. I guess you deserve some credit for it. I was the young kid right out of college, and you weren't going to 'take advantage' of me. Although, I might be flattering myself. You were pretty hung up with that little redhead who worked for *Berliner Zeitung*. What was her name?"

"Erica Thiesser."

"Thiesser. That's right. A very appropriate name," Eloise laughed. Fran joined in, then she continued. "If anybody made a mistake it was me. I should have let you know how I felt. It's a mistake I'm not making this time. You know why? Because I'm surer this time. And I hope it shocks you.

"In Bonn, you were a mentor, and a mentor has power over his student. This time I've gotten to know you as a man. A very sensitive man. Most newsmen are either creeps or ghouls. Out on assignment they're forever trying to climb into your bed. That's bad enough until you realize the only reason they want to is because the bars are closed. Or they have so little sense of human compassion they would ask the wife of an astronaut who was trapped in orbit, 'Tell me, Mrs. Smith, how does it feel knowing your husband is slowly strangling out in space?' "

Fran laughed. Eloise laughed in spite of herself. She went on. "You know I'm propositioning you, don't you? I don't want to talk about love. I need you tonight. I don't want to sleep alone. I'm too scared. I want you to be the solution to all my problems, the way you used to be."

"Eloise." Fran's voice was soft. "I wasn't protecting you in Bonn. I thought you weren't the slightest bit interested in me."

"I'm interested now. Let's go to my room. Palma won't be back tonight."

Fran put some coins on the table to cover the check. He and Eloise rose. She had just slipped her arm into his, when they saw Darren and Virgil looking discouraged, enter the dining room.

Eloise whispered into his ear, "I'll leave the door open. Don't be too long."

They were still standing when Darren and Virgil reached the table in response to his wave.

Fran told them about Palma's having called.

"Well, that's fine," Virgil said with obvious relief. "You people stay. I'm beat down to the sod. I'm going up

149

to bed. Now maybe I can get some sleep. That goddam crazy girl."

"I was just leaving, Mr. McCauley. I'll go up with you."

"You're the only sensible one of the bunch," Virgil said.

"Fran'll be right along," Darren said. "I just need something to warm me up."

"We won't be too long," Fran said, nodding to Eloise.

Chapter 16

Virgil was alone in the bedroom. Guilts and fears swarmed around his head like bats. He thought of his granddaughter, off somewhere, away from her family in a strange city.

A hundred pictures began to crowd his head and Virgil suddenly began to feel like a great magnet. Impulses began to flow into him. He tried to stand, but he couldn't. It was the same as the night of the saucer: he was paralyzed. He felt himself absorbing waves of emotion, as though he were sucking them out of the air. His mind had retreated and was carrying him with it. Virgil made one final effort to stand, and fell backwards across his bed.

It was nearly dawn, and Virgil McCauley was blissfully happy. He sat naked at the oilcloth covered table, his hands clasped around a cup of tepid coffee. Hurka and Verlager had passed out in the other rooms with

151

their girls. Virgil's girl, in a flowery orange kimono, was tinkering around the kitchen stove making herself some tea.

She was some chicken: long, dark hair hanging loosely down her back. Dark eyes. She was a humdinger in the hay, too.

Virgil reached back to the pants hanging on the back of another chair. From the pocket he extracted a ten-dollar bill.

"Hey, Monsherry. C'mere," he said.

The woman turned from the stove, smiling. She gingerly transported a glass of steaming tea to the table.

"Oooh, 'iss 'ot!"

She smiled down at Virgil, *zhee Mareen*. She took one of his Sweet Caporals from its pack on the table, lit it, and lovingly handed it to him.

"Nice? Nice?" she giggled.

"Nice," Virgil said tonelessly.

She stood next to him, running her fingers through his hair. Virgil slid his arm around her waist. He pulled her close. He felt as though he were moving in a dream. His hangover had receded, but his mind wasn't clear. He removed the girl's gown. It dropped around her ankles. She stood nude, like a white flower emerging from orange leaves. He ran his hand slowly over her flesh while she continued to stroke his head.

There was no sexual passion in his touch, rather, he seemed to be quietly rejoicing in the health of her body. It seemed somehow out of place that young bodies should be whole, and that they should smell so good. In the hospital, he was living surrounded by seeping wounds and amputations and mutilations, all clouded over by the choking stench of carbolic acid.

He thought of the bodies up at Belleau Woods, smashed into the ground like crushed bugs, and it seemed strange that one could accept without question that bodies should exist, as she did. It had become axiomatic to Virgil that bodies should cause pain, should be exhausted, should be drenched, should be torn.

"You like?" she whispered.

"Yeah, I like. Damn right."

She stood back from his touch and posed like a little girl.

"Here," Virgil said, pointing to the ten-spot on the table, "this is for you. *Pour vous.* Understand?"

She looked at the ten-dollar bill as though the vault of Croesus' treasure had swung open.

"No. OOOh no. Iss too much. *Trop, comprende?*"

"Take it. What the hell, I ain't gonna be needing it pretty soon. You might as well enjoy it."

She came close and touched his hair again. "You go to trench?"

"I go to trench."

"Ver' soon?" she asked sadly.

"Tootsweet, Kiddo."

"Ah, *mon pauve.* Poor boy."

"To hell with that noise."

"I see you again?" she said.

Virgil laughed. "Christ, I hope not."

The woman backed off as though she had been slapped.

" 'Ope not? I no good for you?" she said.

Virgil continued laughing. "No. That's a joke. A joke. *Compree?* I got to meet you because I am in the hospital. Understand? Wounded. The only way I can see you again until the war is over is to get a bullet in me."

She got it. "Oooooh. I 'ope never see you again also."

Again she stepped to Virgil. She pressed her naked belly to his face.

Virgil was in awe of this woman. The war had awakened something in French women that he couldn't begin to understand. He had never seen it at home, but then, the women at home were safe. These women were not. They only had this feeling for guys who were going to the front, as though each woman knew, at a moment like this, he needed more than just getting his ashes

153

hauled. Whatever unspoken need it was, the women understood it immediately.

A doughboy going on leave, or going behind the lines, could wave a fistful of fifties around and never make it. After all, he was on his way home. He was not in danger anymore. Funny ducks, these women. Virgil would have to do a lot more thinking about them.

Suddenly he snapped up straight in his chair. The woman jumped back. His head began to swirl.

"You hokay?" she asked, alarmed.

"Why does everybody keep saying that to me?" he said.

Virgil felt his insides twist as though he were being sucked into a vacuum.

"No!" he shouted as the room darkened. "No!"

He threw his hands out in front of him as he pitched forward onto the table top.

When he opened his eyes, he found he had slipped onto the floor of his Dublin hotel room. Fortunately, he was alone. He sat up, wondering what it meant that he should have relived one of the delicate moments of his life. A moment he hadn't thought about in years.

Chapter 17

*I*n the morning, Palma did not show up early. In fact, she didn't show up at all. Fran and Virgil had finished bacon and eggs. Eloise had had coffee served in her room. They had packed, had cleared their rooms, and were sitting disconsolately around the lobby when Fran was paged to the phone.

Darren, who joined them a few minutes later, seemed to be the only one who was pulled together. Each of the others were withdrawn, worried.

"That was Palma," Fran growled, returning. "Can you believe she's decided not to come back today?"

"Did she tell you where she was?" Virgil asked.

"No."

"Did she say when she intended to show up?" Virgil said.

"No."

"What's wrong with that girl?" Virgil said.

"I don't know, Grampa. Maybe she's reached the end of her rope like the rest of us."

"I think we ought to talk about this," Darren said, shyly.

"What's to talk about?" Fran snapped, as though Darren were probing into personal, family business.

"I think we have a problem on our hands." Darren pulled his chair in front of the others to form a rough circle.

Darren had no sooner said the words when his meaning hit Eloise. "My God! The aliens!"

"I'm sorry to say, I think that's what it is."

"Wow!" Fran whispered. "We were all so deep into ourselves, nobody ever thought of it." He and Eloise looked guiltily at each other.

Fran was sitting on a love seat next to Virgil. The old man touched his grandson's back.

"You ain't the only one, boy."

"We're idiots. All that girl's life she's been a saint, and here, at the first crack, I'm ready to think the worst of her."

"Fran," Eloise said gently, "let's not talk about her as though she's dead. You just talked to her on the phone."

"That don't mean nothing," Virgil said. "I know them aliens. You can be dead and they can make you talk."

He carried the thought no further, but they all felt a chill come over them.

"How did she sound when you talked to her?" Darren asked.

"All right, I guess. Just like herself."

"No buzzing sound? You know what they sound like."

"No, Grampa. She sounded like herself."

"Well," Darren continued, "maybe they haven't done anything to her yet." The "yet" had sneaked out. "And they probably won't, either," Darren said to make up for his gaff. "This may not be as bad as it seems on the surface. I've been giving it a lot of thought since last

156

night. Look at it this way. Suppose this is a tactic to get us to do what we are going to do anyhow. Get it? We never thought they wouldn't come to Dublin, but as long as we're here, we have the same weapon you guys had in New York: a big city with lots of people, and the aliens didn't want to show themselves to them.

"What the aliens want is to get us alone. Right? Really, the only one they want is Mr. McCauley. So what do they do? They kidnap Palma. They let us worry for a while. Then we get a call telling us where we can find her. And that place will be in an isolated section of town.

"They're doing it to force our hand, so they can get Mr. McCauley alone to deprogram him."

Darren looked around. He noted expressions of mild relief instead of gathering panic.

"How do we get her back?" Virgil asked.

"First of all, I think it's important to understand that the aliens probably don't intend to injure Palma. They have no reason to. They're simply using her as a pawn. I think we have to call their bluff."

"What does that mean?"

"All right. Here goes. I think we can't let them distract us from going to my place. They want a confrontation, and I think we all know that, sooner or later, they're going to have it. The only choice we have is to decide on whose terms the confrontation will occur: theirs or ours. If we do it in Dublin, it'll be on their terms; if we do it in Mayo, it'll be on ours."

"Are you saying we should run out and leave Palma here?" Virgil said.

"I guess so, but it's not exactly what it sounds like."

"I don't give a goddam what it sounds like, I ain't running off and leaving my granddaughter to them—things!"

Darren chose his words carefully. "Mr. McCauley, I know how you feel. I. . . ."

"Son, you ain't got the slightest idea how I feel."

157

"What I mean, sir, is that I love Palma, too. I don't think it's any big secret. I'd give my life before I'd see anything happen to Palma. In fact, I'm going to stay here myself. It's not important that I go. It is important that you and Franny go. They won't hurt Palma, but I think they've proven that they'll kill you."

"He's right, Grampa. If we wait for them to go to bring us to their spot, you'll be killed for sure. If we get them to come to Mayo, we'll have a chance of coming out of this as a whole family."

Neither Fran nor Darren, nor Eloise who was sitting quietly, knew the torture inside Virgil. If, as it had been in the beginning, it had been merely fear that kept Virgil running from the aliens, it might by some human compassion, be understandable, and forgivable. But Virgil knew, since that night in the New York restaurant, that he was fighting now to hold on to a possession: to eternal youth and strength. They were clever all right, them aliens. They were now putting him in a spot where he had to choose between eternity for himself, or his granddaughter's life.

No matter what the logic of Darren's argument, and it looked foolproof, how could Virgil run away?

"Mr. McCauley, I want you to understand that I know exactly the kind of game we're into. You've played it before, and so have I. We're betting Palma's life that I'm right. I know they want you badly enough they very nearly killed you. You see, I'm trying to make sense out of a situation that offers no choices at all.

"If we're going to be realistic about this: they've got Palma. If they want to kill her, they can, and we can't do a thing to stop them. We can only bet they won't hurt her while we try to maneuver them into a position where we all have a fighting chance."

"But you're staying here," Fran said.

"It's a good idea, I think, if one of us does. Just in case she really is with a friend, and I'm all wrong. We

158

don't want to have her come back and find we've deserted her."

Fran looked at Eloise. "What do you think?" he asked.

"I think Darren's right. I think we should go. Ever since New York, they've been closing in. This may be the last chance."

"Grampa? What about you?"

"I'll go with whatever you say," Virgil answered.

"Then it's settled, I guess. We go."

The decision, now made, was a weight on each of them, another shove down a black mountain toward an unknown destination.

Chapter 18

The country west of Dublin is horse country. A wide highway, its direction signs written in both English and Irish, pushes its way through pastures, the rises and wells of which are as regular as ocean waves. Off in the distance, white mansions stand among white corral fences, all designed with the precision of a chessboard. Horses, of the most expensive breeds, stand singly, or in groups, bending their powerful necks, tickling their muzzles against the lush grass. Long muscles ripple beneath their coats like undetonated charges. As the car passes, they sometimes lift their heads and observe with unblinking, philosophical eyes.

Further on, the landscape ruffles: the rises become higher, the wells deeper. The cement highway squeezes down to a two-lane tarmac. Woods and fields, streams, meadows, and lakes tumble by, looking like photos from a travel brochure. The white mansions become small and turn to stone. They crowd up to the roadside.

This is vacation country. Among the refugees from the heat of Dublin and London, the car, with its rental plates, draws no attention.

Traveling gets slow as the car picks its way through the towns. On the roads between the towns, you follow the geographical course of least resistance.

Entering the West Country, the day gets older, the shadows grow long. The stone walls along the roadsides begin. The vegetation gets browner. The farms get smaller. The hills hoist themselves up to mountain size. The houses are less colorful, more weathered, stonier, grayer. The sky begins to look too heavy to support itself: it leans on the mountaintops.

Conversation in the car died away as the grimly familiar terrain reappeared. The menace that seemed to crouch behind every hill seemed consistent with Palma's absence from the car.

They arrived at Darren's place with the first purple of evening. As the car pulled up to the huge front porch, Virgil, Fran, and Eloise, each felt as though whatever was to be decided, would be decided there. They stepped out of the car as if they were Roman martyrs being herded to the Coliseum, yet there seemed to be not one gladiator among them.

On the porch, at the door, they were met by the old woman that Darren had told them about: his housekeeper, Libby; and by Darren's dog, Hounie, a medium-sized mixture somewhere between a Beagle and a German Shepherd. Libby had been off visiting a neighbor who was ill, when they were there after the Swinford incident. But she greeted them now with brisk enthusiasm.

Twenty minutes after the car left for Mayo, Darren stood on the corner of Grafton Street trying to formulate some kind of plan. Convinced his theory was correct, he had decided not to simply wait for Palma to show up, if she were going to show up. He would look for her. If, by some mathematically improbable stroke of fortune, he managed to find her, he could short-circuit the aliens two ways.

All he had to do was find Palma.

Pick a city, he thought in his best journalistic cynicism. Any city. Dublin, Ireland, for example, population: half a million. Now look for a needle. A woman. One single human being. A woman who is being held captive, but by some cosmic alien legerdemain doesn't know she is being held. Where do you begin to look?

Would she be locked up? Maybe. In a hotel room or in an apartment? Possibly. If so, the hotel room or apartment would be somewhere near downtown because the aliens would not have had time to make contacts further out. On the other hand, her mind might be the prison in which the woman was being held. That's really the way the aliens would operate.

If she were being held by the mind, the chances are she would believe herself to be free, and would be given a certain bodily freedom, the aliens knowing they could reel her in anytime they wanted. Now: where would a single woman go, thinking herself free in Dublin? Shopping? How many stores and shops are there in the city of Dublin? What is the mathematical chance that the searcher would walk to the right counter of the right floor of the right shop, and find her?

She might walk around, seeing the sights. Trinity, perhaps, or she might go to a park. If so, which park? Those were places she might go during the daylight hours. Where might she go in the evening? Darren felt his bones turn to water as he checked off in his mind all the theaters, movies, restaurants, coffee houses, tea shops, and confectioners.

He started walking in no particular direction. His shoulders slumped. He felt hopeless.

*   *   *

Libby, Darren's old housekeeper, was really named Liberty. Just before she was born her mother had taken a trip to Dublin to see her sister. That had been in nineteen and aught eight. In St. Stephen's Green, mother had heard Jimmy Larkin—God bless him, even if he was a Communist—haranging a crowd about liberty for the Irish workingman. She had been so enchanted by Larkin, that when her daughter was born, hadn't she named her *Liberty*.

Libby was as thin as a rake. She wore a tan blouse. Her dark-brown wool skirt hung shapelessly over her lisle stockings and brown walking shoes. Her hair was a silver helmet, pulled back to a tight bun. Her skin was transluscent and unwrinkled. Flanking a long, hooked nose, her cerulean eyes were as clear as a mountain lake. She still had such energy that she possessively ran the house all by herself.

She installed Fran, Virgil, and Eloise into their rooms with brisk efficiency. A few minutes later, like a mother hen, she gathered them all in the kitchen for "a bite after your trip."

Too long alone in the country, she talked as though she had been wound to the limits of her mainspring.

"Americans are you? Like Mr. Darren. Ah, that's lovely. A fine place, America. Or so I've heard. Not that I've ever been there myself. It's a West Country girl I am, and have never much left it, except for a bit of a holiday now and then. My older sister, Lord have mercy on her soul, emigrated years ago. She lived in Worchester, Massachusetts. Mr. Darren says it's very near Boston. Do you know it? Perhaps you know my sister. Her name by marriage was Carey."

"I don't think I've ever met your sister, but I know Worchester. It's only about thirty miles from where we come from," Fran said, crunching into a thick slice of homemade white bread.

Old Libby nodded approvingly. As she clattered around her kitchen, the dog, sprawled like a seal in the

163

middle of the floor, its nose resting between its two extended paws, followed her with its eyes.

"Isn't she the tramp?" Libby said, indicating the animal. "Waiting for scraps. Sorry to say, I've spoiled her rotten, but with Mr. Darren gone most of the time, it's a pleasure to have company."

"What a lovely kitchen this is, Libby," Eloise said. She was seated next to Fran at the round, wooden table. She had changed into a powder blue dress. She had a dark blue sweater thrown over her shoulders.

"It's these old houses," Lib answered.

"It's so *big*. It's twice the size of the living room in my apartment in New York. It must be a pleasure to work in a kitchen like this. Mine is so small, you bump your head every time you want to get something in a drawer."

Virgil stood at the back door, looking out. The hominess of the kitchen, and Libby, seemed to add another bizarre dimension to a situation already beyond comprehension. How could they be taking their death stance in such surroundings?

Fran listened to Libby and Eloise talk. He guessed Libby must be originally from County Cavan, by the way she pronounced her *esses*. They were liquid and full; and sibulent. My*s*helf, for myself. *Sh*un, for sun.

Virgil remained at the back door. The armies of night were gathering. They rose up the hillsides like a tide. Even the recurring sense of impending loss didn't bother him anymore. The terror too had subsided. He was again coping with the inevitability of death. Yet there was the strangeness. Out there somewhere were alien creatures from a universe so distant that man might not even be able to calculate its distance.

Fran turned his gaze away from the women to his grandfather. He couldn't guess what it was the old man was seeing. Yes, he was the same old man he had always been, but infused with a strange energy. The more he looked, the more his grandfather seemed like

164

a bundle of stretched skin containing some elemental power that threatened to tear loose at any minute.

At Virgil's suggestion, Fran and he checked through Darren's rack of hunting guns. Virgil chose a 30–30 bolt-action rifle.

"You ain't ever used a rifle much, have you?" Virgil asked his grandson.

"Not since I was a kid and Dad used to take me gunning out in the meadows."

"You better take a shotgun. Here, this is a twelve-gage. You can't miss with it. It'll blow a hole in something big enough to drive a car through."

Eloise stood back near the door of the den, watching the two men handle guns, with distaste and fear.

Virgil snapped his rifle around with professional ease, checking the firing pin, testing the bolt. He then filled two paper bags with ammunition; one for Fran, one for himself.

"Well, might as well go have a look around," Virgil said, leading his grandson to the door.

"Before dinner?"

"Daylight lasts 'til ten o'clock this time of year. We got plenty of time for eating," Virgil answered.

As the two men stepped from the porch onto the grass of the deep, damp twilight, Virgil again felt a surge of power. It surprised him. He stopped for a moment, then continued on. Fran, walking a few feet to the left and behind, didn't notice. Virgil felt as though he might be twenty-two years old. He thought he understood now why the power came and went. Whenever he was up against a situation he didn't understand, like the night of the saucer, his power somehow transferred itself from his body to his mind. But now, psyching up for a real scrap, he was sort of on his own ground. The power would remain in his body.

Virgil stopped. He snuffed the air like a coyote. He let his instincts instruct him. He absorbed the smell of wet earth, wet vegetation. His ears, like radar dishes,

165

picked up sounds: the calls of birds, the lonely chanting of the wind, the far-off wa-wa of a truck horn.

"You know, Grampa, I feel silly. I mean, standing here with a shotgun, getting ready to hassle with a race of creatures that have the power to travel between star systems. God knows what kind of weapons they have. We're like savages using spears against machine guns."

Not wanting to be distracted, Virgil said, "An arrow can kill you just as dead as a machine gun."

As Virgil stood there, flushed with power, his shoulders hunched, his elbows and knees flexed, his muscles tightened, he felt like a warrior. Maybe in some previous life, he had been. There was danger, and at this moment, he was eager for it. He felt like General Patton in that movie he had seen on the TV. They're out in this field after a battle, and Patton says, "War: God help me, I love it."

"Grampa, this is crazy. I'm going back into the house," Fran said.

"Wait a minute. We've got to figure out some kind of tactics."

Fran turned, without answering, and headed for the house. Passing through the front door, Fran stepped aside for the dog, who was on her way out. She shot out directly toward Virgil. Her tail wagged furiously.

"Well, Old Girl. It looks like you and me." Virgil started to walk. The dog fell into step with him. "Let's see what kind of a place we've got to defend here."

The great chessboard was out in front of him.

The house was located dead center on twelve acres of woodland, the forward section of which was cleared, and separated from the rest by a chest-high, lichened, stone wall. Virgil's practiced military eye evaluated the topography. The house sat on the crest of a gentle hill. It had a lawn on all four sides. Good. Clear avenues of fire from any spot in the house. To the south and north, the woods were solid trees, shoulder to shoulder, tight

166

up to the walls. To the east, the woods thinned as they sloped down to the road, a driveway bisected them. Behind the house, to the west, the woods faded. The land twisted upward in a series of watercuts through a rocky incline. The high point of the elevation was higher than the house.

"That's not so good, Old Girl," Virgil said thoughtfully. "Anybody on the top of that hill can cover the west side of the house."

Considering the north and south sides, Virgil wished Darren were here. What the hell was in those woods?

"If I were going to attack that house, Old Girl, I'd set my guns up on that hill behind the house to cause a distraction. Then I'd move a couple of platoons right up behind the walls, both north and south. The flankers would have the house in a crossfire, and both midsections of the line would be close enough to rush."

Virgil figured if he would use the woods, so would the aliens. It was too dark for him to go poking around right now. He would love to know what kind of trails cut through them. How many people could move around undetected? How easily?

What about the areas beyond the wood? Were they populated? Or were they open fields?

"See? That's important stuff to know. If there are no people living around there, these aliens will be able to bring their main ship right in close. That won't be too good for us. But if the area is populated, they'll have to leave the ship someplace else and just send a small force.

"You know what I think, Old Hound Dog? I think they need a low, but clear piece of land, so their lights won't be seen too far off. Where would they find a place like that?"

Right there, he thought, looking at the tall hill, which was shouldered up against another hill behind it.

"God, what I'd give to have the old bunch here right

now. I'd put one fire team on the base of that hill to the south and another one to the north, and by God, when that ship landed we'd have them as soon as they stepped out the door."

Maybe Franny was right. Maybe this thing was crazy. How would he defend anything with just himself and Fran and Eloise and Libby?

"You too, Old Hound, you too. I'm not forgetting."

He decided to check with Libby about the woods.

Chapter 19

*D*arren paid off the cab and shuffled into Jury's Hotel. The inordinate expanse of lobby leading to the elevators seemed too much of an ordeal; yet he rejected the idea of stopping off in the bar for a brandy or two before he checked with the desk clerk. He would be sure to meet someone he knew. The hotel had been something of a hangout of his since the days it had been the Intercontinental, before the old Jury's management had bought it over.

"Ah, Mr. Gilroy," a voice said.

Darren stopped. His eyes turned to a lobby sofa flanked on each end by a huge potted plant. Two men were rising. It took Darren a few seconds to run their identities through his mental computer.

"For Pete's sake," he said, "you're Inspector . . . uh?"

"Cready. It's good to see you again."

"Yes, of course. Inspector Cready, from Swinford."

"Perhaps you remember my aide, Detective Daly."

Darren shook hands with both men. "Can I buy you a drink? The bar's right around the corner."

"That's very kind of you, Mr. Gilroy, but the sad truth is we're on duty. There is, however, an alcove hereabout's where we might get cup of tea. In which case, we would be happy to accept your offer."

"On duty? In Dublin? I thought Mayo was your bailiwick," Darren said as the three men found a table, all but enclosed by potted shrubbery.

"A rather special project," Cready said.

They made small talk until the tea was served.

"Each day," Cready said of the profusion of plant life, "this lobby becomes more like the Royal Hiberian. Apparently the manager does not believe that agriculture is an outdoor activity."

Darren laughed for the first time all day.

Cready took a sip of his tea. "Now to business," he said. "I spoke a bit ago about a special project."

Darren smiled.

"You are that special project, Mr. Gilroy. You and the McCauley family. You'll forgive me if I'm blunt about it."

"Us? I don't understand. What have we done? Are we under suspicion?" Darren asked, in a cool, even voice.

Cready looked to his partner. "I was only saying to Mr. Daly a moment before you arrived that we would have to be careful dealing with you. That you were a chap that has been around the corner, so to speak. It appears you have anticipated us." He sucked on his pipe. "The next logical step is to talk quite openly with you."

Darren saw through the game. This part was called take-them-into-your-confidence-so-they-don't-get-their-defenses-up.

"Inspector, you're playing, and it's going to get us nowhere in a hurry. Look, I'm a foreign national working in this country, which means that neither my employer nor I can afford any trouble from the government. If I'm under any kind of suspicion please tell me, so I can get it straightened out."

"Fair enough," Cready said. "When my partner and I left Swinford to come to Dublin we were, quite honestly, on your tail, as you say in your American motion pictures. I did not think then, nor do I think now, that you told us the entire truth of what happened the night your car was burned. You are suspected of nothing. We've looked you up. You've been in Ireland a long while and there's not the slightest stain against you.

"Since that time—since the time we came to Dublin—we have reason to believe that you might be the victims of some violence. We have agreed that we will be honest with each other. Now, I'm sitting with you man-to-man, Mr. Gilroy and I'm asking you to tell me all the exact details of what happened to you that night in Mayo."

"I guess I couldn't ask for anything plainer than that," Darren said.

Cready nodded. His young assistant sat expressionless.

"Okay. I'll tell you all about it. God knows, I may end up in a mental hospital for it."

Darren told them as much of the story as he personally knew. It was now his turn to respect their professionalism: no change of expression indicated what was going through their mind as he talked.

"Okay. That's it," Darren said, waiting for some sort of judgment.

Cready sucked his pipe once more. "You needn't concern yourself about Miss McCauley. She's quite safe. She's up in her room at this moment packing her suitcases. Had you not appeared, we were planning to take her to Mayo. Now that you are, we'll be glad to save you the expense of renting another car. Of course, you'll come along with us. There are a number of things that remain to be discussed."

"Palma's all right! You found her! Christ, that's great! Thank God for that!"

171

"Now, Mr. Gilroy, there may be more to this than. . . ."

Before Cready could finish, Palma came sweeping into the alcove, beaming. Darren leaped to his feet. He rushed to her and threw his arms around her.

"You really are okay. This is great!" he gushed in a burst of breath.

"Oh, Darren; good, fine, wonderful! Better than anything you can imagine!"

The two policemen, perplexed, caught each other's eyes.

Dinner was a funereal affair. Libby rustled around, loading the table with steaming boiled beef, boiled potatoes, candied carrots, brussels sprouts, bowls of bright yellow butter, freshly baked soda bread, still hot. Next to the beef sat a platter of sliced salami, spiced ham, liverwurst, and cheese. She hovered over Eloise, Fran, and Virgil, urging them to "have a bit of this."

Fran and Eloise ate in silence. Virgil shoveled it in. Libby was amazed that a man eight years her senior could have such a youthful appetite. As she was amazed at the turgidity of his flesh. Between mouthfuls he questioned Libby about the wooded areas. As she spoke, Virgil translated into terms of his military necessity.

She said the woods weren't very extensive. They ran about two or three hundred yards both ways from the wall. She confirmed that the house was pretty isolated.

"There's only the Higgins, them about a mile off. And the Garitys in the other direction."

Most of the land was rolling sheep pasture. She couldn't remember there being anything in the north woods, except maybe a fairy ring. Not that she was likely to be traipsing about the woods at her age, but it seemed to her the south woods had a rather large byre, a shelter for animals, a storehouse for implements. A narrow path ran to it from the driveway.

As Fran smoked his cigarette after dinner, Virgil laid out the situation, and his plans for defense.

He shoved his plate aside. With the end tine of a clean fork he made impressions into the tablecloth, an impromptu map.

"We could do a lot if we had a lot of people, but we ain't got a lot of people. We got three and we're gonna have to do with them. Just like the goddam Marine Corps. As I see it, we got five places we really ought to keep covered. Since we only got three people, two have got to go by the boards. Three places are absolutely for sure. Here, at the base of the hill behind the house. Here, along the path leading from the driveway to that byre. And on the front lawn, keeping an eye on both of the walls.

"Fran, you take the base of the hill. I'll take the path. And Eloise, you take the front lawn. Get yourself a spot up by the porch. It's high enough. And keep a lookout along the walls.

"That way, whoever spots the aliens first will fire off a round and that will be a signal for us to converge on that spot. We'll give those bastards a fight."

"Am I expected to carry a gun?" Eloise said, disbelieving.

"Hell, yes. I'll get you that .22 long rifle Darren has. I'll show you how to use it."

"But, Mr. McCauley, I couldn't use a gun. I'm terrified of them."

"You ain't half as terrified as them spacemen are gonna be," Virgil said.

"Mr. McCauley," Eloise said firmly, "I don't know how this is going to sound, but I have to tell you I don't approve of guns."

Virgil looked at the young woman as though she had suddenly turned into a talking alligator. His face then clouded over. When he spoke, he spoke evenly.

"I guess I know what you're saying to me. I guess I've read it often enough in the newspapers. And God

173

knows, you've taken more chances for this family than we'd have any right to ask in a thousand years. But it's us against them. In this war there ain't no 'alternative service.' We got two choices: we either stay and fight, or we get up and leave."

There was a moment's silence. "Grampa, that's crazy," Fran said.

"That's the second time tonight you've said that to me. Let me tell you: it ain't as crazy as it sounds. I ain't as big an old fool as you think I am. I know we're in a tough spot. I heard what you said about arrows against machine guns, but you know, Son, we got one thing in our favor: surprise. Them aliens know we're smart enough to figure out the odds. They think we'll consider all the angles, then lay down because we know we can't win.

"Well, wars are sometimes won by guys who don't know they can't win. If I got this figured right, them aliens are gonna be cocky. The last thing on this earth they're gonna expect when they open the doors of their spaceship is a face full of buckshot."

As he had before, Virgil swayed them with his rhetoric.

Virgil folded his napkin preparatory to leaving the table. "We might as well get to it," he said. He felt Hounie rest her nose on his leg. Virgil laughed. "Don't worry. I ain't forgetting you. You can patrol the path with me."

The byre was a squat stone structure, square, flat-roofed, shorter and lower than a cottage. Three sides were solid stone, the other was open. A low wall hooked around the open end to form a tiny corral.

One blanket folded beneath him, Virgil sat propped against the corral wall. At the slightest sound, he could command a view of the path for twenty or thirty yards in each direction. Hounie nosed around.

"That's the way the pros do it, Hounie. To hell with

174

the first general order. Nobody in his right mind walks a post in a military manner. You find a spot where you can hide, from which you can see everything. You're all for that, ain't you, girl?"

Like every professional soldier, Virgil felt a certain mechanical ease in the preparations for battle, and a certain competence in actual combat. It was these long hours of boredom that eroded the best of them. The waiting. Nothing to do until the enemy made the first move.

Here on Darren's estate, as on a thousand battlefields, these hours were filled with dreams. Charlie Verlager was always planning this date he was going to have with a chicken he met in Washington, DC. Some planned the house they were going to build. They could tell you about it nail by nail. Young John Wicker, who was killed in a naval bombardment on the Canal, was going to open this bicycle shop. He could tell you about every model he planned to carry.

Now that the lonely hours were upon him, Virgil thought about the changes that had come over him. If things had worked out differently, it could have been the most precious thing he owned. But Palma was more important. So before this night, or tomorrow night was over, he would either be flat on his face dead. Or he would be deprogramed.

He figured he owed that much to Palma. Mainly because he had been so blind about her. He had never thought of her as a person in her own right. She had been there after his son and his wife had been killed in the car crash and had just sort of taken over as the woman of the house. Virgil had accepted it as he accepted rain in the springtime. It was only since Franny had come home this time that he had begun to really look at Palma. She wasn't a kid anymore. She was a full-grown woman who life had somehow passed by as she spent her time taking care of him.

Tonight, Virgil was staking his life for Palma's life.

175

That was little enough. He wished the stakes were higher on the other side. He would give up heaven itself if it would not only spare Palma's life but give her all the things she wanted: a husband, a home, children.

Virgil looked around him in the darkness, the wind beginning to chill him. "Come on, you bastards. Let's get this over with."

Hounie, lying next to the old man, looked up at him.

"Don't pay no attention to me," he said. "I'm like you: an old dog sitting at his master's feet." Virgil looked up to the sky and said, "Amen."

Fran, wrapped tightly in a blanket, had worked himself into a hole. The coldness seeped through to him until he felt he was becoming part of the earth. The hill rose up to the left of him. From where he lay he had an excellent view of the backside of the hill. As he had seen the Marines at Khe San do it, during his first overseas assignment, he lay the shotgun out in front of him on the rim of the hole. Next to it, a neat row of shells, arranged for easy access. It had been comparatively easy for him in Nam: the other guys were going to do the killing, he just had to take notes.

This time it was his turn. He wondered what it would be like to point the gun at a living being. To pull the trigger. To watch the being fly to pieces. Would these aliens scream, as humans screamed? Would they shatter and bleed as humans did?

He reached his hand to the gun and felt the icy barrel. A shudder began at the tip of all his extremities and worked its way to a knot in his midsection.

Fran was suddenly jarred out of his reverie! What was that? The snap of a dry leaf? A footstep? Whatever it was, it had come from behind him. He grabbed the shotgun and swung around with it. There it was again! Beneath the sound of the wind, like an underwater current, he heard something working its way along the

176

base of the hill. His finger tightened on the trigger, the muzzle was pointed directly at the sound!

"Fran? Fran?" said a small voice, almost a part of the wind. "Where are you? It's me, Eloise."

Fran's breath whooshed out in a monumental sigh of relief. "Over here. Over here," he said.

Eloise appeared, magically, out of the darkness. She dropped on the ground next to him. She worked her arms around him and kissed him. Her lips were cold.

"Good Christ," he said after they had parted, "what the hell are you wandering around in the dark for? I'm so trigger happy I could have blown your head off!"

"That sounds like an old movie cliche. Oooh, I'm cold. I should have worn a heavier sweater."

He opened his blanket and pulled her in, then tugged it down behind her. She pressed against him, shuddering deliciously for several moments, then she lay still.

"I wanted to be alone with you. I had to be."

"You're supposed to be guarding the front of the house. What if the aliens decide to come through there?"

"I couldn't help it," she said. "I'm scared. I don't want to be alone."

"I'm kind of scared myself," Fran said.

They cuddled under his blanket like puppies. They twisted and turned and tugged. At this moment they were aware of nothing but each other. No matter how it ended, they needed each other too much right now. Already the devils of the night were deserting them.

"I feel like a teenager," Eloise giggled.

"Me, too."

They began passionate kissing and fondling, saying silly things that teenagers say. "I'm really not that kind of girl." "You won't respect me in the morning." "Yes, I will. Honest." "I hope you don't think I do this with everybody." All accompanied by giggles.

In time they quieted down. The silliness stopped and their kisses became burning coals. They lay full-length, pressing tightly against each other. They were no

177

longer aware of the cold. For endless minutes they managed to blot out the night, and the fear.

Fran held Eloise's head in the crook of his arm. "I can't wait any longer," he rasped.

"I know."

He tried to remove her clothing, but in his excitement, his hands were useless.

"Let me," she whispered.

The two of them shuffled awkwardly under the blanket. Fran's blood turned to lava when he realized she was removing her jeans. He remembered the hundreds of times the movement of her behind under those jeans had excited him in the office, how many times he had wished to see her take them off.

"You haven't even started to undress," she chided him. "I thought you were in a hurry."

The touch of her naked flesh on his, the tickling of her hair, drove Fran wild. He struggled with her. When at last he was steeped in her flesh, she had to manage him as though he were a machine. She at first slowed his frantic tempo, establishing a coaxing rhythm beneath him. She could have wished for a man more controlled, but there was no denying the thrill of his animal desire.

The blanket became too warm for them. They poked their legs out into the cooling air, the sweat of his chest and shoulders soaked his clothing. Eloise turned on her side, drawing her legs up to the fetal position.

"You may like cold air, but I don't," she smiled. "I'll have to remember that about you."

The night did its work quickly. In another moment he was back under the blanket with her.

"You're right," he said. "And you're also looking smug."

"A woman's privilege," she said.

Fran drew the blanket over his head. He drew her head, too, into their own private world. Their universe was now closed to the extent of their senses.

178

"I feel better. Do you?" she asked, as she felt for his face with her finger tips, and kissed him.

"Mnnn!"

"Fran! Wake up!"

Fran had no idea how long he had slept before he felt Eloise's jarring hand. He said something unintelligible.

"Listen," she said.

Eloise jumped from the blanket and quickly danced herself into her jeans, while Fran sat up, reaching for the gun. He cocked his ears. Off in the distance, from the direction of the house, he heard the high pitch of a woman's voice. Calling? Screaming? Probably Libby.

Eloise pecked him a kiss. "I've got to go." Before he could say a word, she disappeared into the darkness.

He, too, struggled into his clothes. He was on his way toward the house when three rifle shots blurted. They were sharp popping sounds. A .22. The rifle was Eloise's.

Fran raced as fast as the darkness permitted. He arrived at the porch about the same time as his grandfather and Hounie.

"What happened?" Fran shouted.

"It's Palma! They've found Palma and she's all right!" Eloise called back.

Fran and Virgil, stopped side by side at the base of the porch stairs, were suddenly stricken by hysterical laughter.

"Darren just called. Palma's all right. They'll be leaving Dublin in the morning," said Eloise, beaming.

"We were wrong!" Virgil shouted to heaven. "We were wrong! The aliens never had Palma at all! Thank God. We were wrong!"

Chapter 20

Certain Irish households, still imbued with the spirit of the old days, serve high tea at four in the afternoon. It is more than a status symbol. It is a ritual midway between the English Mass and a kabuki play. The meal consists of quartered sandwiches, cheese, fruit, crackers, cake, and of course, tea; it is also the stomach's great bulwark against a social custom that dictates one shall not eat dinner until ten o'clock at night.

The Draconian Miss Liberty Powers, born during the labor pains of a revolution and named for its ideal, was no slave of custom, but when Palma, Darren, and the two policemen arrived the next day at noon, high tea was ready. It followed immediately upon the heels of jubilant kisses and embraces. Libby seated her guests. She began with bottles of wine.

"Well, I certainly wasn't captured by *anybody*. I went back to the hotel because it was time to go back. If I'd known all this was going on, I'd have gone back sooner.

You can't know how sorry I am that I worried everybody."

Palma, however, looked anything but penitent. She had bought new clothes. She had had her hair done. She had had a facial and a manicure. She had never looked better. Even her figure looked fuller and more shapely. She was grateful for the joyous reception. When she had met Officers Cready and Daly on her way back to the hotel, she didn't know how she would be received. Everybody had been just wonderful to her.

Just wait until she told them the news! Wouldn't it shock them right out of their shoes? Not right now, though. There was too much confusion. She would wait until the moment was perfect.

As soon as the group had settled down, Virgil felt it was time to get back to business. He explained the situation to them. Fran, who expected his grandfather to be pitied, was surprised that the other men, especially the two policemen agreed with him.

"They've been straight with us," Darren said to Fran and Virgil, "so I told them everything. Apparently they don't think I'm off my rocker."

Cready smiled. "It's true, I've learned in life, that there are more things in heaven and earth than are dreamed of. If you follow my meaning."

"I couldn't be happier," Virgil exulted. "Now we can really give them aliens what-for. We're not spread out anymore. We've got everybody right here. And we've got people. Now we can cover all the bases."

Two hours went by.

"If you'll bring your luggage from the car, I'll see to getting you set up in bedrooms," Libby said after having made some order out of the table.

The men were about to comply when Virgil faced Libby.

"Lib, let me ask you to do us a personal favor. We know how hard you work to keep the house orderly but just this once I have to mess it up on you. You may not have understood what we were talking about a while ago, but it's real important that we all stay together. The ladies can go upstairs, but the men have to be together, so we're gonna stay right here in the living room. Okay?"

"Where in the name of God will you sleep?"

"Right here. There are three couches, and that should be plenty. If you'd bring us some pillows and blankets, that would be great."

Libby, seeing *her* house being disrupted was a volcano inside. She looked to Darren for support. When he nodded agreement with Virgil, Libby turned to the women and guided them toward the stairs. "You two will live like civilized people," she grumped. Disappearing up the stairs, having long since accepted the idea that all men are at least slightly insane, growled, "Hmpf. And them with good Christian beds to sleep in."

For another hour the men discussed tactics.

In the end they did little more than refine Virgil's original plan.

"Another thing," Darren said. "It's a good idea to have everybody scatter around in case those bastards decide to pull the same trip they pulled on us in the car the other night. So, if they use that laser on the house, there'll be nobody in it."

The others nodded.

"That does bring up the question of the old woman, doesn't it?" young Daly said.

"The old woman?" said Virgil.

"She's scarcely able to be patrolling about in the night. If she's in the house, and the house is destroyed, it won't be quite empty, will it?"

"He's right," Virgil said. "I never thought of that last night."

"She's got a friend who lives about a mile down the road. I could run her down there. Give her some kind of an excuse."

182

"Higgins?" Virgil asked.

"That's right. How did you know?"

"If you're going to run her any place, you'd better hurry." Fran, who had risen from the group around the coffee table to stretch his legs, was standing at the window. "It's turning into a mean-looking day."

The clouds, herded in from the sea, had piled up during the past few hours like heaps of dirty wool. The wind had sharpened. The daylight had been cut to the intensity of dusk. A roll of thunder put an exclamation point to Fran's words.

Hounie pressed herself against Virgil's leg. The old man absently patted her head. "Well," he said, "this'll either make things easier or harder. I wonder what the aliens think of thunderstorms."

Virgil's calling it a thunderstorm seemed almost an understatement. It was so dark it might have been an eclipse of the moon. The thunder shivered the roof. Rain battered against the window. Waterspouts on the eaves were disgorging water as heavy as freshets.

Libby made more tea, and served it on the coffee table. There was silence, and the smoking of many cigarettes.

"What a day," Darren said. "I'm glad we left Dublin when we did. Can you imagine being caught in this muck?"

Virgil grunted. The two policemen nodded.

"You really think we'll see those aliens tonight?" Fran asked his grandfather.

"If we do, it'll be their chance to pull a surprise."

"I don't think we have to worry. I think we have the night off," Darren said.

"That's what Rommel said when the bad weather hit Normandy Beach," said Virgil.

"Maybe they're afraid of the lightning. Maybe it would damage their ship," Fran said.

Palma, who had been napping upstairs, made her grand entrance before Virgil could answer. She seemed

183

not the slightest bit depressed by the turn in weather. She had changed into a new tan dress with a tight bodice and a pleated skirt. She wore new shoes. Her hair was fluffed, and hung down to her shoulders. Eloise followed behind like an escort.

Palma's presence changed the tenor of the room. Soon there were compliments for her and laughter all around.

Palma wallowed in the attention. From where she sat at the coffee table, the room was gathered around her. She realized this was the moment to drop her big news.

"You're looking well put together," Fran said to her. "You make the rest of us look like a bunch of frontiersmen."

Palma beamed appreciatively. "If you keep talking like that, I'll begin to think you want me to cook for you."

"Aw, come on," Fran said.

"What's with the new duds?" Virgil asked, proud of his granddaughter. "You inherit some money I don't know about?"

She grinned impishly. "I don't tell you everything. But," she said, with just a hint of suspense in her voice, "I will if you're good."

"Goddammit, woman, you've been sitting on some kind of secret like a hen sittin' on an egg. Now what the hell is it?"

Palma giggled uncontrollably.

"What would you say, if I told you your granddaughter is *engaged?*"

There was a moment of stunned silence. Cready and Daly seemingly the most stunned of all. Then a bedlam of congratulations broke out. All amid great dollops of laughter. The whos, whats, whens, and hows tumbled over each other.

"Oh, he's wonderful. I'm dying to have you meet him. He wouldn't come along because he thought this was a

184

family affair. You know, I didn't tell him about the flying saucer or anything. I don't want him thinking I'm crazy. His name is Padraic, that's Irish for Patrick."

Accompanied by interjected questions, she told the whole story.

She had left the hotel to do some shopping. Just about noontime she started feeling faint so she stopped in front of one of the stores. When she had opened her eyes, there he was. Oh, he was strong and charming and handsome—but not too handsome. She didn't like men who were too handsome. Anyhow, he was just perfect! Practically word for word she recreated their conversation in the tea shop. Somehow the afternoon had just faded away. He hadn't wanted to leave her, so he asked her to go to the theater and dinner with him. What a dinner: martinis, Chicken Kiev, wine.

Fran winced inside, remembering the conversation after the martinis. She must have been at the restaurant when she called.

That night, after dinner, she brushed over completely. They were walking in the park the next afternoon, after lunch when they knew they were in love. And he asked her to marry him! She had left him after tea, promising to return to Dublin to introduce him to her family right after the business in County Mayo was straightened out.

"What does this bird do for a living?" Virgil asked.

"He runs a book store."

The conversation continued to flow around her as though she were a rock and they the sea, as though she were the sun toward which every flower inclined.

It was her moment. The moment she had waited for all her life! Libby became a fountain of trite advice. Eloise stood quietly and grinned rather fatuously. The men made jokes. That is, all but the two policemen did. They sat silently. Their faces were professionally expressionless.

"Will you be living in Ireland, or will the two of you move back to the States?" Eloise asked.

"I don't know yet. We haven't talked about it, but a wife has to live where her husband is," Palma said smugly.

Fran stood up, banging noisily on his teacup with his spoon.

"All right. All right," he said to the group. "Somebody's got to stand up here and say a few words to the bride-to-be." Fran lifted his teacup. He thought for a few seconds then said, "I give you the bride-to-be: my sister, Palma Marie McCauley. The world is made up of two kinds of people: the givers and the takers. Let's drink to Padraic, a guy who was lucky enough to get a woman to whom I literally owe everything I am today; a woman who has transmuted *giving* into an art form as precious as truth, beauty, and nobility."

There was an instant of silent appreciation, then loud applause and cheers.

Palma threw her arms around her brother. "Did you really just make that up?" she said, her eyes brimming.

"No. I've been thinking about it for a long time. I was just waiting for the right opportunity to say it."

"Oh, Franny, I love you!"

The spontaneous party lifted the tension inside, but outside, the storm raged with unabated vigor. Each knew that it was past time for them to tend to their duties outside, but no one wanted to be the first to suggest Palma's party should come to an end.

Palma was huddled with her grandfather, her brother, Eloise, and Libby. Darren, who had kept up a good front during the fuss about Palma getting married, gradually drifted from the little knot. He walked to his gun case. He fiddled idly with a couple of statuettes, symbols of his proficiency, that stood on the case mantle. He felt a great sense of loss. Granted, he really had no reason to think so, but he had always sort of taken it for granted that one day he and Palma would marry. Well, that's what comes of being the guy who always bides his time, he thought. He guessed no woman waits forever. What the hell even made him think Palma was waiting for him in the first place? He had the idea that Palma's not getting married all these years had something to do with him. What a damned fool!

"I'm going upstairs for a minute," he said to his friends.

No one responded.

Darren walked through the narrow hallway toward the back of the house. From there, there was another, narrower staircase leading upstairs. As he reached the upstairs corridor, he realized someone was in the hallway outside the bathroom. They were talking in soft voices. It was Cready and Daly.

"But how long before we do something?" Daly was saying.

"I haven't a clue," his superior officer answered. "Wouldn't it be grand to *do* something. What do you suggest we do? I haven't a clue about that, either."

"There must be something. Health laws. Something. The entire family is a pack of bloody lunatics. The old man: him plotting out shooting space people. For the love of God! And that daughter. What about her?"

"Indeed," said Cready, "what about her? True, the lot of them are insane. Unfortunately, there's no law against being insane, unless you become dangerous."

"What do we do? Just go on playing along?"

"Under the circumstances, I see no other choice. Do you?"

The two men turned, and descended the stairs, back to the living room. Darren leaned back against the stairway wall. So, the *Garda* didn't believe him after all. And what in the immortal hell were they talking about? "And the daughter?" they had said as though the answer to the question had been self-evident. What about the daughter?

* * *

It would have been hard to tell, as he sat on the sofa surrounded by his family, letting the women do most of the talking, that Virgil was engaged in something that resembled a silent prayer of thanksgiving.

Everything had worked out just hunky-dory. Now that Palma was back with them, the aliens had no bargaining point. He had been willing to give up his newly acquired power, his promise of eternal youth, to save her, but now he didn't have to. If those aliens wanted it back they were going to have to fight like hell for it.

Virgil felt like a man, who, for the second time, had been reprieved. Inside, he felt the joyous agreement of vibrations: through his tissue, through his brain.

"I've been meaning to ask you," Libby said, away from the young people, "is it a fact that you're really eighty years old?"

"Guilty," Virgil smiled.

"It's a wondrous thing," she said. "If someone was to tell me you was sixty, wouldn't I believe them."

Eloise, too, drifted away from the crowd. Up in her room, alone, she stood at the window watching the fury. The party downstairs had started thoughts, like puppies, rushing around in her mind. None of them would stand still long enough to be clearly seen; they brushed here, they scampered there.

God! she thought, what victims of our training we are! For so many centuries, marriage been the glittering Olympus of every woman, and her wedding day the biggest day. Was there no way to avoid it? Eloise had chosen the life she had to live, and she had been—was—happy with it. She had studied hard for a certain kind of work. Why had there been no cheers? No congratulations? No toasts? When she had gotten the job she had always wanted?

Would a woman who won the Pulitzer Prize receive half the adulation of someone like Palma who had somehow managed to trade what God had given her into a wedding ring? Yet, damn it! Even she, swept up in the emotions of the moment, found herself envying Palma!

What could the estimable Padraic have seen in Palma, that Fran could not see in her? Eloise was certainly smarter, certainly better looking, and probably better in bed than Palma was. No question that Palma had slept with her knight in shining armor, as Eloise had slept with Fran. Palma had a lifetime commitment to show for it. What did she have?

Suppose she wanted to, would Fran marry her? Was there really any value to sex? Was it something you gave because the time was right? Or was it something you bargained with? If Fran did want to marry her, did she want to get married?

Oh, Jesus. She hated herself for all these crazy thoughts. We are such suckers for a wedding, she thought.

The room became too small. She had to breathe fresh air. She threw on her raincoat. She felt a sudden affinity for the angry storm.

She took the back stairway down to the first floor. There was a door, she discovered, that took her into the cellar. From there she could use the side exit. Outside, she closed the cellar door with great difficulty, the wind nearly tore it from her hands. She fought the wind around the house to a little sheltered spot she had discovered earlier. The cold rain lashed her face. The iciness was a joy after the closeness of her room.

"I hate to be the one to say this," Virgil said, "but we'll have to pick this party up again later. I think it's time we got out to our posts."

Palma did not seem disappointed. Her party had been a roaring success. It was slowly dying of its own weight. To tell the truth, the emotional jolt of it had rather drained her.

"Okay," she said, "but I expect a much better performance at the reception."

"You can count on that," he said. Looking to the two policemen. "You ready?" They nodded. "You've got your own weapons, right? Wait a minute. No. I'd better get you something bigger, just in case."

Virgil started toward the gun case where the shotguns were kept when the air was torn by a scream of terror from outside the house. Another. Virgil skidded to a stop. The other men in the room jumped to their feet. Palma's head snapped toward the door.

"What the hell was that?" Virgil said.

"Sounds like the scream of a woman," Cready said.

"From the front lawn," said Fran.

They started for the door. Halfway there, the front door smashed open! Standing there, outlined by a blue flash of lightning, stood two men dressed in black! Over their shoulders they could see Eloise being dragged away by two other men!

Chapter 21

*B*oth strangers pointed box-like hand weapons at the occupants. Without warning, Darren and Detective Daly hurled themselves forward. The air vibrated. Darren and Daly were slammed backward. Their bodies were flung to the floor, where they lay unconscious like tangled puppets.

The strangers promptly rounded up Cready, Virgil, Palma, Fran, and Libby in the area of the coffee table; forced them to sit down. They paid no attention to Libby's terrified shrieking.

"Please do not compel us to use more force," one of the aliens said in that buzzing voice that was a hideous approximation of the human sound.

The aliens cautiously moved closer to the coffee table.

"What the hell have you done with Eloise?" Fran said.

"Do not fear. The woman will not be injured. Nor will you."

Darren and Daly sat up. They, too, were herded into the circle. This was the first time either of them had seen the aliens. Or felt the sting of their auras. Darren grimaced. Daly, and at a distance, Cready, were stunned almost to paralysis. They looked at each other vainly for comprehension.

The aliens assured them again that Eloise was safe, and they were also. "It is, however, necessary that we communicate with each other. We hoped you would accept us on our word back on your own continent. It is obvious that your race has reached a level of progress in which explanations are necessary."

The humans were frozen rigid in their chairs.

"How could we accept you at your word," Fran managed to ask, "when you hate us so much? It's so intense we can feel it every time you come near us."

The aliens consulted each other. They exchanged thoughts and some buzzing utterances.

"For reasons you will more fully understand later, the reaction you feel to our presence is quite natural. We are another race, more fully evolved. We are from a star system beyond even the imaginations of your most dreaming scientists. Because we bear no resemblance to you, either physically or psychically, we appear before you in forms taken from probings of your consciousness. Forms you find acceptable, but disturbing. Such biologic advancement is disturbing to you on every level of your perception. Can you understand?"

Silence.

"Although your race has evolved beyond the R-8 stage," the alien continued, "we are sufficiently advanced so that you would perceive in us the same threat that all other creatures on your planet perceive in you. It is perfectly natural. The 'hate' you perceive is an externalization of your own fear."

Virgil then broke from his mesmerization.

"What about that dog?" he said, nodding toward the

192

cringing beast lying among them. "He ain't afraid of me."

"That is true. As you perceive it. It does not mean, however, that the dog feels no sense of threat. The dog's species came to terms with yours many generations ago. It has had millenia to learn instinctively that it is possible for him to coexist. How would this species respond if you were to meet it in its wild state?"

"That's what we are, huh? In our wild state?" Darren said.

"Precisely."

"That's just great." Darren's irony was lost.

"You say you really don't look like what you seem to be," said Fran. "What do you look like?"

"You are not prepared for that."

"Why don't we cut out all this garbage," Fran said. "How am I supposed to sit here talking to a couple of kidnappers who are holding my girl." No one, including Fran himself, noted how he had referred to Eloise.

"Yeah, and I don't like negotiating with a guy who has a gun pointed at my head," Virgil said.

"Within the timespan of an hour of your time we shall have completed the process we came here to perform. You shall all be safe. We shall return to our routine business."

"Well, goddammit, you got us. What the hell are you waiting for?" said Virgil.

The alien seemed to consider his reply.

"You have evolved into an unexpectedly bellicose species. Although you have scarcely frustrated us, you have made the mission troublesome. It is necessary for us to explain certain things to you so your cooperation with us is willing and understanding. Mr. McCauley has inadvertently become the carrier of a disease which threatens your entire race. It is necessary that this entire group undergo medical decontamination. We have already lost much time because you did not understand."

"That's why you grabbed off Eloise, huh?" said Fran.

"Precisely. There is an aphorism of your culture which states: 'sometimes you must choke a dog to give him medicine.' "

"What do you mean 'entire group'? I thought it was me you were after," Virgil said.

"In the beginning, yes."

Each of the humans looked at each other.

"Try to imagine," the alien began his explanation, "a time in your history so long ago that your race did not exist in its present form. Imagine your race so primitive that it was one with the other animal species that populated the planet: creatures living in a state of nature whose perception was limited almost entirely to survival instincts."

"Naked apes?" Darren sneered.

"Precisely," said the alien, with scientific logic. "Try to imagine another race in the multi-warp system that you have come to call *space*. Imagine this race sending out exploratory probes with the intention of colonizing, very much as your European countries did five centuries ago.

"In the same sense that your Christopher Columbus 'discovered' the north and south continents of America, imagine this other race 'discovering' your planet.

"Is it not an axiom of colonization that the primitive natives be formed and educated to the ways of their 'discoverers'?"

"To make exploitation simpler," said Darren.

"Precisely," said the alien. "There was one particular circumstance that arose in the case of the explorers that discovered your primitive ancestors. When the members of the crew mated with the females of your ancestors, an event which always occurs when explorers are isolated for long periods of time, they discovered that the offspring formed a decidedly superior race, with their paternal proginators specialized per-

194

ception, the type of super-animal consciousness that allows itself to think outside nature."

"Wait a minute," said Fran, "are you saying that modern-day humans are half indigenous animals and half spaceman?"

"Yes."

It took a moment for that to sink in.

"Consider:" the alien went on, "that you are separate from every other animal on your planet, not because you have intelligence, and the ability to communicate. Many species possess that. You are different in your ability to consider yourself outside nature. Yours is the only race that has ever set out to 'conquer' nature. The other species cannot even make that conception. That is your heritage from us."

" '. . . Made in the image and likeness, and that likeness is mainly in the spirit?' " Darren quoted, bitterly.

"You mean, you're not aliens at all: you're our parents?" Fran's voice sounded as though it was stepping up toward hysteria.

The alien nodded. He continued, "As you say, *parents*. Like all parents we wished to raise our children well. When that particular expedition, the one that discovered your planet, returned home and told the Technological Council that it had left behind halfbreed children, it was decided as a matter of official policy that you be educated to the level of your parents.

"As you can easily imagine, it was not possible for us to have you attend classes, year after year, century after century, millenium after millenium. It was decided to set up a series of Evolution Capsules, and then to abandon the planet, so that you would be able to develop the nuances of a unique culture, rather than be influenced by personal contact. All, of course, within the framework of the Evolution Capsules."

"Evolution Capsules?" Fran asked.

"Yes. A series of pre-set energy generating devices

designed to stimulate your brain power to a certain level of development as you became psychologically ready for it. The overall effect was to bring your species, step by step, up the evolutionary ladder."

"Are you soft?" Virgil said. "You mean to tell me that people are what they are because of a lot of capsules you guys left laying around?"

"*Left around* is rather an oversimplification. They were carefully timed and hidden, set to go off in proper order. For example, the first capsule would be designed to teach you how to use your newly acquired brain power for personal survival. I need not remind you that in what you call your prehistoric ages, humanity was scarcely a physically dominant, ferocious species. At a time when species survival was a matter of brute strength, you can see where humanity, by every mathematical probability, was very likely to be extinguished. The next capsule would be designed to show your species how it could ease the rigors of existence by mutual cooperation, teaching you to live and hunt in packs, rather than individually. Once this had been established species-wide, you would then be shown how agriculture and husbandry would give you the stability upon which to build a civilization. And so on until you are capable of the ultimate step."

"Bullshit," said Virgil.

Unruffled, the alien continued. "Consider: do you think it an accident that all cultures on your planet began in one spot and then spread? According to your own histories: 'civilization' began in the Nile Valley, and spread outward in concentric circles. This phase taught advanced agriculture, primitive mathematics, arts, and crafts. In successive order, advancements on these subjects blossomed in Sumer, Ur, and so on. A millenium later, advanced arts grew in the islands of Greece. Simultaneous advances occurred in Cathay. Later, law and organization blossomed in Rome, and spread outward. Granted, this too is an oversimplification, but please concede that there has been a rather obvious relationship between human evolution and geography."

The seven humans were silent.

"You have reached a stage we call R–8. It is a stage of physical development and rational thought process. R–10, two steps away, is the top level of *physical* development. At which point, you will begin developing the potential of your minds. For example, at the moment, mind and body are linked inseparably together. You have discovered that it is possible to travel in what you call space. You have developed a primitive form of transportation. In having your minds and bodies linked together, you have automatically set the limitations of your technology. You see, you must reach a day when the transportation of your physical bodies becomes impossible because you will never find a way to exceed the speed of light with physical weight."

"At which point, another capsule will go off," Darren said.

"Yes. Precisely. It will mark the end of your physical development, and the beginning of your mental. The final goal of which will be to bring you to the point where the body is useful only as a brain case. Herein, is the current problem."

The humans sat like befuddled pupils.

"If physical structure," the alien went on, "becomes the victim of its own limitations, doesn't it follow that everything else physical does? Is it not logical to assume that your species can transcend its limitations only by moving into another realm? In this case the mental, or if you prefer, the psychic? To continue with our analogy of space travel, transportation, at your stage of development, is still a matter of moving both the body and the mind because body and mind are both necessary at present for that state you call consciousness. Suppose it were possible to imbue the mind with total consciousness? And the body become little more than a shell? Would not transportation become simply a matter of moving a weightless 'consciousness' instead of a body?

"In a very primitive form, you already possess the ability. You call it ESP.

"Think of the possibilities. Now you can travel only to those points to which your bodies can be moved. Mentally, you could transport your consciousness in a microsecond of thought. No spot in the universe, an area you cannot even conceive, would be inaccessible to you.

"At the moment you can only cogently communicate with your own species because your communication is a matter of transferring symbols of thought. In the future you will be able to communicate with every species because you will be communicating the thought itself."

Virgil, Fran, Palma, Darren, Libby, and the two policemen were hypnotized as the alien painted the future.

"Bearing in mind the iron structure of scientific logic, does it not follow that the future series of capsules would deal with mind development? Continue asking yourselves, what would be the logical goal of ultimate psychic evolution? Would it not be the power to create? The power to bring into existence any reality by a mere act of will?"

"My God," Fran said.

"Precisely. Your God. Do you not already have the concept?"

"Yes, but this is the power of God: creation. Not the power of humans."

"In a sense that you do not yet understand, this power of creation is quite properly accredited to That which you call God. The history of your race is a step by step progression from the Darkness—Oriental Humans have such a concept—to gradually brightening degrees of light. You have never understood the light until you

198

have stood under it. Do you not have such an idea in the theological teachings of your Western culture? Is it illogical to assume that a primitive being, for the sake of preserving his sanity, would ascribe to a higher power an ability which he himself had seen operate, yet was completely beyond his knowledge?"

The alien thought deeply for a minute. The ensuing silence was crushing. He then went on, "The capsule which was to have taken you into the final series of mental development is the source of your 'plague.' It is set to detonate in your year 12,000 AD. Unfortunately, through a fault in its physical mechanism, it went off accidentally a week ago. Fortunately, only one human being was in the vicinity and had been affected by it before repairs could be made."

"You mean . . . ?" Virgil began.

"I am sorry to say, yes," the alien said. "Your totally unprepared brain center was exposed to a power for which it will not be capable of coping with until humanity has progressed for another ten thousand years. Being unable to adjust, the brain will eventually be destroyed."

"Sweet Jesus," said Virgil, lifting both hands to his temples.

"So that is the 'plague'?" Fran said.

"Yes. The victim finds himself capable of acts which he cannot psychologically accept. His very tissues, not only his comprehension, are driven beyond the boundaries of endurance. In a short time, they will disintegrate."

"I don't understand," Virgil said.

"Once you had been exposed to the radiation of the capsule that day in the pine forest, you had the power of God-like creativity. By an act of will you could bring into existence, or eliminate from existence, any object you desired.

"Briefly, let me say that there is no objective reality, in the sense that your science has taught you. It is only

199

the first step of advanced evolution. It permits you to conceive a world so that you may establish your position in it. What you consider the objective 'world' is not reality. It is a perception of sense organs designed only to reflect, not analyze. There is only personal reality. Which is to say, there are as many 'worlds' to be perceived as there are minds to perceive them.

"One day, with your new power, you decided the only world that could make you happy was the time spectrum in which you spent a period of your youth. Unknown to you, the power within you allowed you to bring that world into existence. It was, for you, reality. At such a callow stage of development, you could not long sustain your creative ability, so you seemed to be moving back and forth between what you considered the real world, and what the world thought fantasy.

"You remember the night in the field when you first arrived in this country? It puzzled you that, in a sense, you repelled us. What you actually did, quite unconsciously in your fear, was to create a world in which we did not exist. Since contact requires that we be part of *your* perception, we had no choice but to withdraw.

"You have observed already that your brain, with or without your volition, continues to create the worlds of your desire. It will continue until your brain cells are burned out. You will reach a transition stage you have come to think of as death."

"Holy Christ," said Virgil.

"And you people have been chasing us around the world to save Grampa's life?" Fran said.

"No. It's more complicated than that, isn't it?" Darren guessed.

"Yes," the alien said. "The single infection is only part of the problem. If you recall, I called it a plague. A plague is by its definition communicable.

"The purpose of the capsules is to 'infect' all humanity. When it detonates, a capsule affects one person. This person infects all who come into contact with him.

Then the newly infected also infect those who come into contact with them until at last the 'infection' becomes worldwide."

Virgil sat upright in his chair. At last, things had become clear to him. He had resisted the aliens out of motives ranging from fear to greed. He had not known what he possessed, he had had only the vaguest notions. Nor had he known what he was giving up if he submitted: his granddaughter, when he thought she was being held by them; his life—an eternity of health and youth, a fountain of youth, an El Dorado for which a thousand conquistadores had perished. Now he knew everything was illusion. If he continued to resist the aliens, he chose a gradually disintegrating dream world which would lead to quick death; if he submitted to them, he earned the plain ol' human right to a normal death of old age.

Yet the alien had said *all* reality was illusion. Virgil at that moment wished he were a more educated man, like his grandson or Darren. Perhaps then he could deal with the philosophical implications. For all the grand worlds that might be open to him at this juncture, he knew he would choose normality. If it were illusion, it was at least an illusion that he was used to.

All fear of the aliens, all greed passed from the old man now.

"Well, goddammit," Virgil said, "you came here to deprogram me, let's get to it. I'll go with you right now. Let's do it before I give the infection to someone else."

Palma seemed to wake up from a dream. For the first time since the aliens had entered the house, she responded.

"Gramps, no!" she said, throwing her arms around the old man.

"Don't worry about me, Honey. I'll be okay one way or the other," Virgil said.

A sudden tension came over Darren. He spoke to the alien as he tenderly disengaged Palma from her grandfather. "Look, she's exhausted and she's scared. Would it be okay with you guys if she went upstairs to her room to rest while we get all the arrangements made? Don't worry. We're not running anymore. We came here to get this straightened out once and for all and that's what we're doing." By his own mental power, Darren seemed to be trying to tell the aliens something beyond his words.

The alien assented. Libby took the sobbing Palma upstairs to her bedroom. "Don't worry, for God's sake, I'll be all right," Virgil called after her.

When at last Darren, Fran, Virgil, Cready, and Daly were alone with the aliens, Darren spoke. "Thanks for that," he said. "I don't know if you people have anything that resembles human emotions, but you were understanding enough to know that we have them."

"You communicated your need to us," the alien said.

"A couple of minutes ago, Mr. McCauley said for you to deprogram before he infected anyone else with his power. It's not true, is it? He has already infected someone." Darren indicated the upstairs with a motion of his head.

"That is correct," he said, the alien being as emotionlessly logical as usual. "She began to manifest two days ago in the city."

Fran and Virgil were turned to stone.

The alien continued, "Once exposed to a human who has been radiated, other humans immediately acquire the ability to create. The capability, however, manifests itself first in those with the strongest desires. McCauley," the alien nodded to Virgil, "was obsessed with the desire to relive certain portions of his life, hence he mustered the necessary psychic power to do so. The female upstairs is obsessed with mating and reproduction, hence the ability to create her personal reality."

"What the hell are you saying?" Fran said.

Softly, kindly, Darren spoke. "Franny, he's saying

that Palma isn't engaged. She is not going to be married. There isn't even a man named Padraic." Unexpectedly, he turned to the two policemen. "That's right, isn't it?"

Cready's voice was husky. "I don't know how you found out, but that's right."

"I put two and two together," Darren said.

"No engagement? No wedding?" said Fran.

"I'm afraid that's right," said Cready.

Virgil exploded. "You're all nuts!"

"I just did some guessing. I don't know any of the facts. Tell him," Darren said to Cready.

"I'm truly sorry, Mr. McCauley. I didn't understand until a few minutes ago. A few minutes before these, uh, gentlemen came into the house, Detective Daly and I had a meeting in which we had decided that . . . well, we couldn't decide how to handle it. Every word, sir, that Palma told you about a gentleman named Padraic, about dinner, and the theater, and the rendezvous, and the engagement were simply not true."

Virgil collapsed in his chair as though all the air had been pumped out of him.

The Inspector went on, "For reasons which I will explain to you later, Mr. Daly and I followed you to Dublin. We were waiting outside the hotel when your granddaughter left alone that morning. I assigned Mr. Daly to follow her while I remained at the hotel.

"He followed her about. She did the usual female things. She shopped. She bought a thing here and there. Around noon it was, near St. Anne's Avenue, she fainted. Mr. Daly helped her to his car. She was taken to the local hospital and when she recovered she seemed determined to set off again. She was so sure of herself that we could find no excuse to detain her. But she was alone during the period she says these events occurred to her. And that's the truth."

"No engagement. No wedding," Virgil muttered to himself.

"Oh, my God. Poor Palma," Fran said.

"The time has arrived," the alien said. "We must begin." He held out his hand to Virgil. "You first. Then the female upstairs."

Virgil sprang from the chair! He howled like a wounded animal. "No!" The shock of his response caused the alien to take a step backward. "No." he bellowed again. "No deprograming Palma! I don't care if it's all in her head! It's real to her and that's the way it's going to stay! That girl has lived her whole life for this moment. It's the thing she wants more than anything else on earth! And by God, she's going to have it!

"I was dumb once before. I let her sacrifice it for me. I ain't doing it this time. I ain't letting nobody else do it, either. I ain't as smart as you guys. I don't claim to know what's real and what's not real. All's I know is that my granddaughter is happy for the first time since she got out of high school, and she's gonna stay that way."

"But, Mr. McCauley," Darren said, "it's all a dream. She could die from it."

"I don't give a damn if it's a dream or if it ain't. It's real enough for her. Didn't you see the expression on her face? How the hell you gonna take that away from her? Well, I ain't, and you ain't, nobody ain't.

"And if she dies from it, by God, she's gonna die happy!"

"I'm afraid that's quite impossible," one of the aliens said. "We must go now." The alien extended his hand again. "Come."

Before a single blink of cogent thought could pass among any of them, Virgil had a shotgun in his hand. It had been propped unnoticed against his chair. The room suddenly rocked with the roar of two almost simultaneous explosions! The weapon belched its glut of double-O buckshot in a searing flash of fire! The aliens, both of them, flew backwards!

Chapter 22

*T*he men heard a scream behind them. They turned to see Palma standing at the base of the stairs. Virgil wondered how long she had been there. How much she had heard. His question was immediately answered by the expression on her face. The way the light slanted across her face, it looked like a death mask. She was a corpse: denuded of feelings, hopes, dreams, aspirations; devoid of a future, numbed by the past, consigned to a present of icy indifference. Only the beating of her heart indicated the spark that vitalized her.

"Honey, don't you listen to these crazy bastards. They don't know what the hell they're talking about," Virgil rasped. The other men were stunned. Only Fran turned his head away from the look on his sister's face. He turned to the two aliens who were piled like garbage on the floor.

"Oh, Jesus. Oh, Jesus," he wailed.

The others turned.

The two corpses on the floor, pounded to mush by the shotgun blast at such close range, first began to twitch, then flop like wounded seals, making obscene slurping sounds as they did. The bodies themselves, and the chunks that had been torn from them, began to glow with a dull luminescence. The humanoid flesh shivered and slowly dissolved! In its place, making a nightmare travesty of the human clothing, took shape two starborn abominations of such transcendent ugliness as might drive the human mind to the comfort of insanity! As close as words might describe them, they resembled magenta, pulpy lobsters, from the backs of which grew hundreds of sensor stalks crowned with cancerian eyes!

"Saints in Heaven," Cready whispered. "That's what they really look like."

The glow around the corpses grew increasingly brighter. Like electrical impulses, great plumes of chromatic lunacy rose from them and whirled like dust devils! The two howling mad, malignant rainbows swirled faster and faster, tighter and tighter! When at last they gathered themselves into two columns, each emitted a piercing feedback screech and winked out.

The assumed flesh of the alien bodies, now abandoned, began to melt into a single pool of oozing putrescence. A stink rose from it as ghastly as a hundred open graves. The observers gagged.

"They were almost pure energy," Darren whispered to no one in particular.

"Ah, Sweet Jesus. Sweet Jesus," chanted young Daly, nearly out of his mind.

Eloise's clothes were dripping, tattered rags. Her hair was plastered to her. Her voice was raw from screaming. The aliens, one on each side of her, each with one of her arms locked in his, dragged her through the woods. Even in the semi-numbness of her terror she screamed as branches whipped her, sharp rocks underfoot tore at her feet and ankles.

They reached a tiny stone hut that would have been invisible in the darkness had it not been for a pulsating, purplish glow from inside. She was dragged through the gate of a low corral. She realized this was the byre that Mr. McCauley had talked about. He had been sure the aliens would use it if they found it. How right he had been!

She was pitched through the open end of the hut with such force that she toppled and rolled on the floor.

Like a trapped animal, she raised herself up on her elbows, with wild eyes she looked around. What should have been a backwoods repository for primitive farm implements was instead a dazzling science laboratory. The intricacy of it took her breath away.

Along one wall stood a tall device that blinked and clicked like a computer face. Along another was a device which resembled an oversized, glass-domed birdbath. A bank of toggles and lights impressed into a stainless steel face stood against the other. In the middle of the room, looking ominous, was a small stand upon which was fixed what seemed to be a huge, inverted test tube with bands of copper tape set in strange designs upon it. It was easily big enough to hold a human being.

The two aliens stood in the hut opening like nightmare creatures, against the backdrop of slashing rain.

Eloise was suddenly jerked to her feet! Some power within her head had done it. An instant later, her hands, helpless within the power of whatever it was that was playing the motor switches of her brain, began removing her stained, tattered clothing. Even as her own hands stripped her, she screamed her protests.

Like a puppet, her legs became functional. They wobbled her out the door of the hut into the downpour and stopped. She stood as though in a shower. Once cleansed of the mud and bloodstains of her recent ordeal, her legs carried her back inside. One of the aliens had unlocked the giant test tube and had turned it down on its side, so that now it lay horizontal.

"Noooooo!!!" she screamed, as she realized the power within her brain was moving her toward the opening of the tube!

Howling all the while, a volition greater than her own forced her to crawl into the tube. The two aliens easily righted the device until, clasped tightly within the tube's glassy textured embrace, she was standing upright: naked and exposed to her enemies. Her terror was so great that it stole her voice from her.

One of the two aliens stared expressionlessly at her while the other stood at the left-hand bank of instruments. He began playing them like a keyboard. The deck beneath Eloise's feet began to hum. The vibrations on her feet were maddening. Then panic set in as the plate began to glow. Unconsciously, she associated such a glow with an increase in heat, for in fact, it was glowing like white-hot metal, even though there was no temperature change. Instinctively, she tried to escape it. Her legs were too confined to move them. She succeeded only in hopping up and down on her toes.

An instant later, the plate beneath her feet was no longer important. A rending pain, blindingly, whiteningly, dug into her head. It felt like a terminal migraine. She screamed vainly into the dull air around her.

The pain passed. Fingers eager and hungry began to tickle her brain. Soon they seemed to find what they were looking for. They gently tugged. They milked her as clever fingers milk a cow. A grayness gathered around her. A weakness suffused her body. She knew she was going to faint. She mustered every shred of strength to stave it off, all to no avail. She felt herself slipping—slipping. In the last moment of consciousness she hallucinated: beside each of the two men outside her transparent coffin a cloud of iridescent color gathered and spun. Each cocked his head as though listening.

That's all she remembered.

Back at the house, the frozen tableau came to life. Fran first, then the detectives, then Darren, finally Virgil, who was still staring at his devastated grand-daughter.

"We've ripped it this time," Fran said. "We'd better get moving around. Come on, Grampa. You wanted a fight, you got one. Those guys will be back for blood this time."

Fran could see that his Grandfather had not really recovered from the shock of seeing Palma's despair on her face. His wakefulness was the wakefulness of a trance. Fran could not shake him loose.

He snatched the shotgun from the old man's hands.

"Get a shotgun, Darren. You, too," meaning Cready and Daly. "Darren you have more ammo for this, don't you?"

"Yeah. In the gun case. But what the hell are we going to do?"

"First we're going to get Eloise back and then we're going to get the hell out of here. Libby, get a raincoat for yourself and for Palma, then go out to one of the cars. Flop down with her on the floor of the back seat and wait for us."

Libby looked at Darren for confirmation. When he nodded his head, she took off up the stairs for the second floor.

The men each held a shotgun.

"We know we can hurt them. Grampa showed us that. The aliens took Eloise in the direction of the byre. That's where we're going. With the four of us, we can get them."

"Wait a minute," said Darren. "Why should we go running out there? The alien told us that Mr. McCauley has power in his mind. 'An act of will.' Maybe he can free her without our even leaving this room."

"For Christ's sake, Darren, look at him. He's out of

209

it. He doesn't even know what's going on. We'll take him to one of the cars, too."

"Where are we going?" Darren asked.

"What difference does it make? We're not fit to deal with this. Look at us: we're all half-crazy. I don't care if we have to run for the rest of our lives, I don't ever want to face those aliens again."

"Then why . . . ?"

"We have to get Eloise."

Without the slightest warning, Detective Daly cracked. He began sobbing loudly. He dropped the gun in front of him as he slid to his knees. He crumpled in a heap. "Mother of God. Mother of God." He mumbled over and over the one phrase that he hoped would somehow keep him cemented to sanity.

The other men looked with sympathy on the young policeman.

"Let's get moving," Fran said. He was obviously the one in command now. "No. Out the side entrance so they can't see us from the direction of the byre. That's the direction they went in."

One by one, the crippled group worked its way out into the bawling night: the healthy supporting, half-carrying the ill. Libby, the catatonic Palma, and Virgil, the wracked Daly were safely stowed in the two cars. Just as Fran, Darren, and Cready were about to turn away, they realized they had forgotten someone. Outside Virgil's door stood Hounie, her fur dripping, whining loudly.

"For Christ's sake, get in then," Darren growled.

The three men, now alone and armed to the teeth, worked their way around the house toward the north wall, doing their utmost to remain invisible. The storm continued to rage. The rain was a battering sheet of water. The air quivered from the fury of the thunder. The lightning: daggers of fire. In an instant the three men were soaked.

They skittered across the lawn in a direct line for the

210

wall once they had cleared the protection of the house. During a lightning flash they would drop to the ground, in the ensuing blackness, they were up and off again.

They reached the wall. Their hair was plastered to their foreheads. Water dripped from their chins. They scrunched down, working their way slowly toward the driveway entrance. The smell of wet, fecund earth was as heavy as mist.

Inside, each was driven by his own fears, especially Fran, whose imagination nipped at him with images of the things the aliens might be doing to Eloise. He wished, too, he could handle situations like this as well as his grandfather did. Fran had no experience in things military, yet here he was leading two men in a desperate effort to do that which no human being had ever done before. The solid blackness of the woods stood against them as a symbol: impenetrable, elder, and deadly.

"Okay," Fran whispered as they reached the tarmac of the driveway, as he gathered the other two around him. "This is the entrance to the path, isn't it, Darren?"

"Yeah. You'd better let me go first. I know this area better than you do. This path approaches the byre from the left. When we get to a bend about halfway down, I'll stop and give you a signal. You two cut through the woods to the left. Inspector, you go out about a hundred metres in a straight line, Franny, you go about fifty. That'll put each of us in a line facing the byre from the same direction. That way, we won't be shooting each other."

"And let's not start shooting until we know where Eloise is," Fran said.

"Right," Darren said.

Into the maw they went, Darren leading the way, Fran next, then Cready.

Darren kept his eyes moving as he stalked: lifting his feet high, setting them down softly. In this moment of cataclysmic danger, an internal beam scanned the banks of his personal emotions. He felt as though he were a kid again: on a snowy Saturday morning whizzing down Belmont Street on his sled, beyond his control, responding to the laws of gravity. He knew that he was in the woods, but he was not sure why. To save Eloise, of course, was the excuse, but what was his reason? Palma.

Darren reached the bend in the road. He knew he could give no signal in the darkness, so he waited until the others caught up with him.

"Hey, Darren," Fran whispered harshly, "have you seen anything in the trees?"

"Like what?"

"I'm not sure. I only get quick glimpses of it. It looks a little like those floating colors that came up from the bodies back at the house. Does that make sense?"

"I didn't see anything," Darren said.

Cready said, "I believe I saw the same thing. It's hard to say exactly what it is."

"Christ," Fran said. "Nothing makes sense: the woods, the storm, the aliens, the capsules. Maybe we're all crazy. Or maybe we're asleep and we'll wake up and this whole thing will be a bad dream."

"You guys take off that way. This is the place I told you about," Darren said. "I'll give you a couple of minutes, then I'll start moving forward again. The byre is only about fifty metres up this way."

Fran and Cready had only taken a few steps into the woods, when the air suddenly began to hum! A bolt of energy smashed Cready in the chest! He flew backwards as though hit with a baseball bat!

"Scatter!" Darren shouted, and flopped full-length into the mud of the path. Like a crab he scuttled forward.

Fran tore into the woods.

A piercing light sliced through the treetops from the direction of the byre. The rain refracted it into a hundred thousand diamond pinpoints.

"Jesus! They know!" Fran said to himself, seeming to shout over the flush of panic as he ripped through the undergrowth. The air around him hummed again: probing, searching. Fran dropped to the ground. Madly he crawled on hands and knees.

Fran heard the roar of Darren's gun. Thank God he was still alive! Fran continued to slash forward. He heard Darren's gun again. This time he heard the clatter of pellets on stone. The alien's weapons hummed, and Fran immediately realized what Darren was doing: ad-libbing like a pro. He had them shooting at him. He was diverting them so Fran could get in close. Fran increased speed until, quite surprisingly, he bumped headfirst into the stone corral.

Fran slowly lifted his head over the wall. He realized he had stumbled into a minute of ineffable luck. Two aliens, and he saw no others, were standing at the gate of the corral, their weapon boxes in their hands and their backs turned to him. Best of all, Eloise was nowhere near them.

He brought the gun up and fired twice! His first shot tore away one alien's head. The other, his box at the ready, spun around. The second shot caught him full in the face like a hammer!

Another shot from Darren's gun raked the top of the byre.

"Darren! Darren! It's me. Fran! Don't shoot. I got 'em! Don't shoot!"

Fran leaped the corral wall. He straightened up about the same instant Darren came flying in through the gate. He glanced for a moment at the torn aliens.

"Any more around?" he gasped.

"I don't see any."

Inside the door of the byre both men stopped, amazed at the sight of all the scientific equipment. On the ground, next to a device that looked like an overgrown test tube they found Eloise. She was naked. She had

213

pulled her knees tightly to her chest. She was totally still.

"Oh, God," Fran said, touching the iciness of her skin. "I think she's dead."

"No, she's not," said Darren. "She's breathing. I can see it. She's unconscious and she's cold. Darren hurriedly stripped off his raincoat, putting it on her while Fran got over his initial shock. "C'mon," Darren said. "Let's get her out of here. We don't know how many aliens are around."

Fran slung the young woman over his shoulder, following Darren out the door.

They were astonished to see Cready, whom they were sure had been killed, sitting up, rubbing his chest.

Cready followed the other two men out of the woods and across the lawn. An instant later they arrived at the cars.

Darren took the wheel of one, Fran the other. Virgil, Palma, and Eloise were in Fran's car; Cready, Daly, and Libby in the other. In the excitement, Hounie hopped out into the rain. The door slammed before she had a chance to get back in.

The engines of both cars roared to life. The cars rolled slowly down the driveway, leaving the sad-eyed dog behind.

Darren, at the wheel of the lead car, maneuvered carefully, without lights, just in case there should be more aliens around. Fran was right behind him. They rolled along that way until they reached the approach to the main road.

Darren suddenly exulted.

"We beat them, Libby! Goddammit, we beat them!"

The windshield wipers and the rain beat against the car like applause. One final dip before the road.

"Thank God, we made it," Darren said.

In that instant the sky opened up. The light of a hundred suns blinded both drivers. The electrical sys-

214

tems of both cars died. The source of the light, a cylindrical object overhead, beamed with cyclopian fury. Before the passengers in the cars could so much as register their horror, a surge of power struck them. They froze for a moment in quivering rigidity, then toppled, unconscious.

Chapter 23

Morning parted the rumpled curtain of hills and dawned silent and gray. Not the gray of neutrality, but the gray of nothingness, space, of void. It had stopped raining. The exhausted clouds rested on the earth, trailing tattered coattails from the hilltops. Like fog, they spread out over the fields.

Palma was the first to wake up. For one delicious moment, her mind stretched. Then her eyes flicked open. Oh God, she thought.

She was lying on the living room floor of Darren's house. A pillow had been stuffed beneath her head, a blanket thrown over her. Scattered around her, sleeping peacefully were Gramps, Franny, Darren, Libby, Eloise, Inspector Cready, and Detective Daly.

She untangled herself and sat up. The memories of last night flowed back to her. She stood quickly, the blanket falling around her feet. As she did so she felt that her clothes were somehow, indefinably, wrong.

More than the normal disorder of having slept in them. It felt as though they had been removed, then replaced in a way she wouldn't have done it.

She shook Virgil.

"Gramps. Gramps. Are you all right? Wake up."

"What the hell's wrong with you?" he mumbled sleepily. Then, "Oh, Christ. . . ."

In a minute they were all awake, yawning and stretching. Libby, scandalized at having slept on a couch all night in her clothes, hurried upstairs. She was soon followed by Palma and Eloise who had realized that she was still naked under Darren's raincoat.

The men sat silently, each coming from the depths of sleep in his own way. Darren rubbed his eyes. Virgil lit a Camel, saying, "Can't breathe 'til I've had that first cigarette." Fran ran his fingers through his hair. The men were stiff from their unaccustomed sleeping place.

Darren, who had done a lot of camping, wondered why he didn't feel chilly from sleeping in wet clothes.

A minute later Libby returned downstairs and began clattering a coffee pot in the kitchen.

"We might as well talk about it. It ain't gonna do no good standing around like a bunch of clams."

Libby distributed coffee. "'Tis left over from last night, but it will do 'til I get some fresh made." She knew her Americans.

"It's all over, isn't it? I mean, we've all been deprogramed while we were knocked out. I can tell. I feel different. Look at us all. We're right back to where we used to be."

Palma and Eloise, freshly dressed, came down the stairs quietly. They were served coffee. They found themselves a seat among the men.

"It seems you're right," said Cready.

"And all that running around was for nothing," Fran said. "They got us without even ruffling their hair."

"I wouldn't say that," Darren said. "We gave them a good fight. We got four of them. We're all still alive."

"It's a reward they gave us," Eloise said, unexpectedly.

"Oh?" said Fran.

"I found out when I was being deprogramed last night. It was no mistake to run, Honey," she said to Fran. "They would have killed us. They planned to right from the beginning."

"That ain't what they told me," said Virgil.

"Death doesn't mean the same thing to them as it means to us," she said. "To them, with their highly advanced evolution, death is merely a kind of electric transference from one body into another. Bodies are nothing more than just storehouses for the brain generators. They don't know what death means to us." Back to Fran. "Because we ran; because we fought them every inch of the way, they decided if our lives are that important, they'd let us keep them. I found that out just before I passed out in that awful tube. They said something about giving us other things, but I fainted before I could find out.

"We didn't really kill anyone. We just made their current bodies uninhabitable. They intended to kill me last night, but the two we shot here appeared in the byre in the form of that color they use. That's the conversation I heard. Heard it in my mind, if you know what I mean.

"The reason they set up in the byre was to experiment on ways to deprogram us without killing us."

"Are they gone now?" Palma asked.

Eloise nodded. "They're gone."

There was a long pause, everyone alone with his own thoughts. Virgil sat in the big chair. Hounie rested her muzzle on his knee while he patted her head.

"They're gone," Fran said, "as though they'd never been here."

"What the hell are we moping about? If it's all over, let's say *Thank God*. We're all alive. Some of us lost more than others. We're still alive. That's more than any of us expected. Instead of being happy we're sitting here with our chins on the ground."

His words seemed to be all they needed, yet each one had been afraid to say them himself. No one wanted to believe that the great renunciation of death had been announced: superstitious fear that by saying the words the reality would cease to exist. It had been death they had fought against these last days. Now they were breathless with relief. Life and death had struggled, and life, with all its disappointments, had won.

Freshly made coffee was brought in. Libby was surprised to see one single smile start then spread from face to face like a forest fire.

Outside, a beam of sun even broke through the clouds.

Chapter 24

*F*ran was alone in his room that night. There was a knock on the door.

"Mind if I come in?" Eloise said.

"No," he smiled. "You can help me drink some of this coffee. Libby makes it for me as though I'll die if I have to go an hour without some."

"Thank you, but I think I'll pass. I just checked the mirror and noticed that I'm turning a decided mocha brown from the coffee I've already had."

They sat side by side on the bed.

"I decided to dress for dinner," she said. "How do you like it?"

She had pulled her hair back into a tight bun. She wore an ankle-length, lace-trimmed linen dress, straight out of the last century. She had done her eyes. Her lipstick was pale.

"You look great," he said.

"I thought I ought to make some effort for our going-away party."

220

"Oh?" Fran said.

She laughed. "Oh? What do you think we talked about all through tea?"

"I know," he said. "It's just that I never *really* thought about it."

"You're getting more like Darren every day," she said.

"That sounds kind of swampy. You mean I'm keeping my mouth shut when I should be talking?"

"I don't know," Eloise said. "Mr. Cready and Darren told me what a fuss you made when the aliens had me captured. You were willing to risk everybody's life to get me back. Darren says you even called me your girl. Tomorrow afternoon I'll be in Shannon. Tomorrow night I'll be on a plane heading back for New York. It seems to me we have some things we ought to say to each other."

"I love you. You know that by now," he said.

"Yes. I know. And I love you, too. What we have to talk about is where we go from here. You and me, as an us."

"Where do you want to go?"

"I don't know."

"Would anything stop you from getting on that airplane?" he asked, knowing the answer.

"I don't think so. I have my job."

"Would you marry me if I asked you?"

"I don't know."

The man and the woman were both staring at their feet.

"So then what are we talking about? I love you and you love me. You're in New York. I'm in Bonn. You visit me on your vacation? I visit you on my vacation? Is that what we've got?"

"Oh, God. I don't know. Why is it always choices? Pick this *or* that? Why can't we just love each other? Why does love always have to mean something else?"

Fran slipped his arm around her. "I don't know

anything, either. Except maybe one thing: I have something now I didn't have before."

They kissed. Their emotion, like their fears, was an aphrodisiac.

"Don't mess my hair," she said, as he pushed her down on the bed. "Oh, the hell with it. Mess my hair if you want to."

Darren was alone on the wide front porch when Palma, dressed to the nines, stepped out.

He walked over to her, took her by the arm and led her to the railing where he had been standing.

She took a deep breath. "It's beautiful," she said.

"It gets like that after a big rain over here. Although that rain yesterday wasn't very typical. That's more like Florida. It's like a cycle: first it rains, then it gets clear and fresh like this."

"What were you thinking about when I came out?" she asked. "You looked deep in thought."

"I was thinking about everything getting back to normal after all—this. Eloise is going back to New York. You and Fran and Mr. McCauley will be leaving tomorrow. The two cops will be going back to work."

Palma laughed. "Ol' Sneaky Franny thought he was going to take us all home, but Gramps and I threatened him until he finally agreed to finish up the vacation. He promised us London and Paris, and, by God, we're going to get it!"

"I'm going to miss you," Darren said.

Palma squeezed his arm. Afterwards, she did not move away.

"What'll you do when you get back home?"

"Oh, the same thing I've always done, I guess."

Silence.

"You don't sound excited about it," Darren said, at last.

"There's not much to get excited about."

"I know. My life isn't a hell of a lot, either."

"I'm going to miss you, too. As far as I'm concerned, the best thing to come out of this trip so far, is the different way I see you."

"Better?" he said.

"Better," she smiled.

Darren took a deep breath. "Do you like Ireland?"

"Of course, it's lovely."

"I mean, do you like it here at this house, and everything?"

"Yes. But I don't exactly know what you mean."

"What I mean is, I've spent my whole life not sticking my neck out as far as you're concerned. Well, I'd rather be rejected than spend the rest of it wondering about what it might have been, you see? I mean, if you're going to miss me, and I'm going to miss you, why should we? Why don't you marry me and stay here?"

"Would you like me to?"

"Oh, for Christmas sake, Palma, you know how I feel."

"I know how you felt when we were kids. Do you still feel that way?" she said.

"Hell, yes."

"All right. I'll marry you, if you want me."

Darren shyly took Palma in his arms. "I'm not Padraic, you know," he said.

"Padraic," she said, "was a dream. Every girl has one."

"I'm not," he said.

"No," she smiled, "you're just the best catch in Ireland."

They kissed, long and hard.

Resting her face against his shoulder afterward, she said, "Only one thing bothers me."

"What?" Darren drew back, concerned.

She smiled again. "Do you think I can get a second engagement party in two days?"

"You know something, Old Girl," Virgil said to Hounie as they walked up the driveway, "I'm glad the whole

223

goddam thing is over." The dog rubbed gleefully against his leg.

"I looked in the mirror before I came out of the house, and, by God, I've put on about twenty years. Guess I was too used to looking the way I did—the other way. It ain't no big loss though. Tomorrow we'll all be taking off and things will get back to normal. Hell, that's the way it ought to be.

"Them aliens was right. We're better off without them goddam 'gifts' of theirs. Now we're all deprogramed and that's good. I couldn't handle all that. And I was just one guy. Then there was Palma: all of us living in our own world. Trying to do things none of us could understand. Playing God.

"Nah, we're better off. Imagine what that would have been like if it had spread over the whole world. You know, Old Girl, I ain't got a hell of a life, and you ain't got a hell of a life, but it's ours. Who needs to see all his dreams come true?"

When they reached the part of the driveway that forked off into the path leading to the byre, the dog started to edge toward it.

"So, it's night and you want to go moseying around? Well, go ahead. I gotta go up to the house. See you later."

Hounie trotted down the darkened path, her tail high, an unaccustomed light glistening in her eyes. Her people had been so concerned with their own affairs that they'd forgotten to feed her. Going on along the path, she ignored the lightness she felt in her head; she concentrated on food. As she reached the big oak tree, her heart jumped. There, looking foggy through her blurred vision, tangled in a vine so that it could not extricate itself, was the biggest, plumpest, most delicious-looking rabbit Hounie had ever seen.